Emma Madison stared at her computer screen. She couldn't believe what she was seeing.

The photo on the fan Web site was of a young Zach Trainer, the lead guitarist and founder of the rock band Freight Train.

With him was a beautiful girl. He had his arm around her, and she was gazing up at him adoringly. The caption read *Zach Trainer and His Singer Girlfriend, Zoe.*

The girl couldn't be anyone but Emma's mother. Emma would have recognized her anywhere. The wildly curly red hair. The face. The smile. Suddenly Emma's heart accelerated.

She stared. Swallowed. The picture had been taken the year before she was born.

Was it possible?

Could Zach Trainer be her father?

Dear Reader,

Well, if there were ever a month that screamed for a good love story—make that six!—February would be it. So here are our Valentine's Day gifts to you from Silhouette Special Edition. Let's start with *The Road to Reunion* by Gina Wilkins, next up in her FAMILY FOUND series. When the beautiful daughter of the couple who raised him tries to get a taciturn cowboy to come home for a family reunion, Kyle Reeves is determined to turn her down. But try getting Molly Walker to take no for an answer! In Marie Ferrarella's *Husbands and Other Strangers,* a woman in a boating accident finds her head injury left her with no permanent effects—except for the fact that she can't seem to recall her husband. In the next installment of our FAMILY BUSINESS continuity, *The Boss and Miss Baxter* by Wendy Warren, an unemployed single mother is offered a job—not to mention a place to live for her and her children—with the grumpy, if gorgeous, man who fired her!

"Who's Your Daddy?" is a question that takes on new meaning when a young woman learns that a rock star is her biological father, that her mother is really in love with his brother—and that she herself can't resist her new father's protégé. Read all about it in *It Runs in the Family* by Patricia Kay, the second in her CALLIE'S CORNER CAFÉ miniseries. *Vermont Valentine,* the conclusion to Kristin Hardy's HOLIDAY HEARTS miniseries, tells the story of the last single Trask brother, Jacob—he's been alone for thirty-six years. But that's about to change, courtesy of the beautiful scientist now doing research on his property. And in Teresa Hill's *A Little Bit Engaged,* a woman who's been a bride-to-be for five years yet never saw fit to actually set a wedding date finds true love where she least expects it—with a pastor.

So keep warm, stay romantic, and we'll see you next month....

Gail Chasan
Senior Editor

Please address questions and book requests to:
Silhouette Reader Service
U.S.: 3010 Walden Ave., P.O. Box 1325, Buffalo, NY 14269
Canadian: P.O. Box 609, Fort Erie, Ont. L2A 5X3

IT RUNS IN THE FAMILY

PATRICIA KAY

Silhouette

SPECIAL EDITION

Published by Silhouette Books

America's Publisher of Contemporary Romance

SILHOUETTE BOOKS

ISBN0-373-24738-9

IT RUNS IN THE FAMILY

This edition published by arrangement with Harlequin Books S.A.

® and TM are trademarks of Harlequin Books S.A., used under license. Trademarks indicated with ® are registered in the United States Patent and Trademark Office, the Canadian Trade Marks Office and in other countries.

Visit Silhouette Books at www.eHarlequin.com

Printed in U.S.A.

PATRICIA KAY,

formerly writing as Trisha Alexander, is the *USA TODAY* bestselling author of more than thirty contemporary romances. She lives in Houston, Texas. To learn more about her, visit her Web site at www.patriciakay.com.

Prologue

Pregnant!

Zoe Madison stared at the pregnancy test stick. It was definitely blue.

How could this have happened?

She had been so careful. Not trusting Zach to take care of prevention, she had seen a doctor and gotten a prescription for birth control pills as soon as she realized theirs was going to be an ongoing relationship.

Obviously, the pills hadn't worked!

What am I going to do?

Zoe thought about Mandy Rogers, the drummer's

girlfriend who had been traveling with the band since before Zoe had been hired on as their singer. Mandy had gotten pregnant a couple of months ago, and Jimmy—the drummer—had insisted she have an abortion. He'd said he was too young to be a father. Besides, what would they do with a baby on the road? Mandy had cried on Zoe's shoulder, and Zoe had felt so sorry for her.

Zoe would never forget how Zach had dismissed the problem when she'd told him about it. He'd shrugged, saying, "Hey, that's the way it goes. It was stupid to let herself get pregnant."

Zoe had wanted to say it took two, that Jimmy had to assume some responsibility for the pregnancy, but she knew it wouldn't have done any good. She would just tick Zach off, and nothing would change.

So she'd kept quiet.

Mandy had had her abortion. But ever since, in unguarded moments, her eyes looked sad and haunted, and Zoe knew she was thinking about her baby, the one who would never be.

As much as Zoe wished she could forget her roots, as much as she wanted nothing to do with her father's hellfire and brimstone philosophy, there was a part of her that knew she could not do what Mandy had done.

The question now was, should she take a chance and tell Zach? Or should she figure out how she was going to manage on her own without involving him?

Zach.

Just saying his name used to fill her with longing. She'd been crazy about him from the first moment she saw him with his long, shining black hair and dreamy gray eyes, his sexy smile and cocky stance.

They'd been together now for six months. Six incredible months filled with music and sex and an intoxicating freedom Zoe had reveled in, because it was so opposite from the world where she'd grown up.

But even in this altered state of bliss, Zoe hadn't been blind to Zach's shortcomings. She was a smart girl. She'd skipped a grade and graduated at the top of her class at the age of seventeen. But Zoe was more than book smart, she instinctively understood people. She always had. So she'd realized from the beginning that Zach was completely and totally self-centered and focused on his music. This fact hadn't bothered Zoe much since he was the center of her world, too, and she had wanted the same things for him he'd wanted for himself.

But now…now things were different. Now she was pregnant. Now she had someone besides herself to think about.

And…if she were being totally honest, she'd admit that lately Zach had sometimes acted impatient. As if he might be getting tired of her. Zoe hadn't wanted to think about it, had pretended she was imagining things, but she knew she wasn't. The truth was, Zach didn't like to be tied down. He wasn't with her for the long haul but for the pleasure of the moment.

She had to face it. What they had wouldn't last much longer. One of these days, she would bore him. And then he would move on.

If I have this baby, I'll have to do it on my own.

But could she?

Sure, she'd left home at seventeen, gone to New York with only seven hundred dollars to her name, and managed to find a job and a place to live before running out of money. And that job—as a clerk in a music store—had led to her audition as a singer with Freight Train, and now, barely past her eighteenth birthday, she was an established member of an up-and-coming band that was beginning to make some really decent money.

But if she had this baby, she'd have to leave the band. She'd have to strike out on her own again, because even if she could swallow her pride and stay, Zach wouldn't want her there—a constant reminder of something he'd prefer to pretend had never happened.

Zoe tried to push down the panic that threatened to take hold. She had to think clearly.

Where could she go? Back to New York?

Zoe swallowed.

She had exactly thirty-three cents over one thousand dollars in her savings account. She should have put aside more, but she hadn't thought she'd need it, so she'd been indulging herself, buying more clothes than she really needed and splurging on some really great shoes.

Would she be as lucky this time as she'd been when she first left home? Would she find a job right away? Would her money last until she did?

And even if it did, how long would she be able to work? And what would she do when she no longer could?

If only she could go home.

But she knew that wasn't possible. Her mother might welcome her, but her father never would. In his eyes, she was a sinner. And sinners had no place in his home.

She was alone.

All alone.

Fear sidled into her heart.

I don't have to make any decisions right this minute. I have some time. I can think about this.

Zoe tried to still the trembling that threatened to overwhelm her as the gravity of her situation sank in. She stuffed the pregnancy stick and the kit it had come in deep into the wastebasket and covered it with wadded up toilet tissue. Then she took several deep breaths and opened the door.

"I thought maybe you fell in."

Zoe blinked.

Zach stood there grinning at her.

Pushing the knowledge of her pregnancy to the back of her mind, she managed a smile she hoped wouldn't give away her inner turmoil. "Sorry."

"No problem, babe. Just wanted to make sure you were okay." Leaning over, he kissed her.

Sometimes Zach could be so sweet, so thoughtful. Maybe she *could* tell him. Maybe she was doing him an injustice. Maybe he really *did* love her. Maybe he would feel different about a baby of his own.

But just then Mandy walked past, and Zach frowned. Once she was out of earshot, he said, "I'm gettin' a little tired of her hangdog look."

And just as quickly as the possibility of telling Zach about the pregnancy had entered her head, it left. He wouldn't be happy about her news. That had been wishful thinking on her part.

And really, could she blame him?

He was only twenty, and the band was just beginning to do well. The next few years would be critical for them. They would be on the road nonstop, building their fan base. They'd work hard and party even harder. Even if what they had *did* survive, that was no life for a child. No life for a family.

For the rest of the day and evening, she thought

about her dilemma. She was still thinking about it that night, after the show, when Zach and the rest of the band and their hangers-on were heading out to get something to eat.

Zoe begged off, pleading a headache.

Zach dropped a casual kiss on her cheek. "Don't wait up," he said. "We'll probably go to Charlie's later."

Charlie's was an after-hours club where musicians congregated for jam sessions that sometimes lasted till dawn.

Once Zach was gone, Zoe got up. Quickly—she didn't trust herself to think too hard about what she was doing, because she might get cold feet—she packed up her belongings. When everything she owned didn't fit into her two suitcases, she appropriated one of Zach's duffel bags. An hour later, she was done.

She looked around their hotel room. For the past three weeks, this had been her home. She considered leaving a note for Zach, then decided not to. There was nothing to say. A clean break was best.

Picking up the phone, she called the front desk. Ten minutes later, the lone bellman—this wasn't a fancy hotel—knocked on the door. After loading her things onto the luggage carrier, they rode the elevator down to the lobby in silence.

"I'll get you a cab," the bellman said. "You stay here. It's cold out there."

Zoe smiled gratefully. Chicago in January was more than cold. It was frigid. The wind cut through you like a knife.

Minutes later, the bellman signaled to her, and Zoe pushed through the revolving doors to join him. She was standing there, shivering as the wind off the lake buffeted her, while the cab driver and bellman loaded her bags into the trunk. Just as they finished, someone touched her shoulder.

"Zoe?"

She whirled around. For a moment, she didn't recognize the tall, good-looking man with the slightly crooked nose who stood there gazing down at her.

Then she blinked.

Omigod.

It was Sam Welch, Zach's older half brother.

"Are you leaving?" he asked.

"Um, I—" At a loss, Zoe couldn't think what to say. Her heart was beating wildly, as if she'd done something wrong.

"Are you okay? Did something happen?"

He frowned. His voice sounded concerned, but that was probably just her ears playing tricks on her. Because she was well aware that Sam didn't like her. He'd made that obvious the few times she'd been in his company.

"I—I have to go," she said, fighting panic.

"But—"

"I have to go." Turning away, she handed the bell-man three dollars. He opened the back door of the cab, and she climbed in.

"Zoe, wait!" Sam called.

But the bellman had already closed her door.

Sam knocked on her window.

Zoe shook her head. "Take me to the bus station," she told the cab driver.

As the cab pulled away from the curb, the last thing Zoe saw was Sam Welch's worried face.

Chapter One

Twenty-three years later...

Emma Madison stared at her computer screen. She couldn't believe what she was seeing.

The photo on the fan Web site was of a young Zach Trainer, the lead guitarist and founder of the rock band Freight Train. Judging by how young he looked, it had been taken at least twenty years ago, Emma figured.

In the photo, Zach Trainer wasn't alone.

With him was a beautiful girl. He had his arm around her, and she was gazing up at him adoringly.

The caption under the photo read: *Zach Trainer and his singer girlfriend Zoe.*

Zoe.

Even though it was almost impossible for Emma to believe, the girl couldn't be anyone but Emma's mother. Emma would have recognized her anywhere. The wildly curly red hair. The face. The smile.

Even if Emma had never seen a picture of her mother when she was young, she'd have known her. But Emma had seen pictures. Many of them. And now there was no doubt in her mind. This Zoe in the photo was her mother.

His singer girlfriend?

Emma was stunned.

If her mother knew Zach Trainer, why hadn't she ever mentioned it? Freight Train was one of the most famous rock bands in the world. How could she not mention knowing him? Especially as both she and Emma were musicians and talked about music all the time.

A singer?

Yes, Emma knew her mother had sung in church and in her high school chorus. And several years ago, her mother had joined a women's choral group.

But this caption implied that she had sung with Zach Trainer's band. Why had she never *told* Emma?

Suddenly, Emma's heart accelerated.

Unless…

Omigod.

Her hand shook as she moved the mouse down through the story, trying to find out exactly when the picture had been taken. Suddenly she spied the date about midway through the article. She stared. Swallowed. The picture had been taken the year before she was born.

Now her heart was beating so hard and so fast, it scared her.

Her mind whirled.

Was it possible?

Could *Zach Trainer* be her father?

She thought about Zach Trainer's almost-black hair. Emma's hair was almost black, too, although hers was curly like her mother's and his was straight.

She thought about his famous gray eyes, which the fan mags were always saying were the color of rain. Emma's eyes were gray, too. And even though no one had ever compared them to the color of rain, that was because no one she knew was given to fanciful images.

And she thought about his musical genius. Emma had always thought she'd inherited her talent and love of music from her mother, who was an accomplished pianist. But maybe Emma's gift—a gift her mother admitted far surpassed her own—had come from another gene pool.

"Zach Trainer," she whispered.

Now she thought about how her mother would never talk about her father. All Emma had ever been told was that her mom had gotten involved with him when she was very young.

"It was a mistake," she'd said. "But I'm not sorry, because I got you out of the whole deal."

She'd always smiled and hugged and kissed Emma after saying that, and Emma knew it was because her mother hadn't wanted her to feel unloved or unwanted.

And Emma never had.

She knew her mother loved her.

And she loved her mother back.

They had a wonderful relationship, except for this one thing. Emma wanted to know her father. She had always felt incomplete. At the very least, she'd wanted to know *who* he was. But no matter how many times Emma questioned her, her mother would never tell her anything more.

Once, when Emma was sixteen and in that stubborn stage where she wouldn't stop pestering when she wanted something, her mother had lost her temper.

"Emma, stop it! You father doesn't even know you exist, and believe me, if he did, it wouldn't make any difference. Now leave it alone."

What she'd said had hurt Emma, and she'd stopped pestering, but she hadn't forgotten.

How could she?

She had a father, and he was out there some-where, and he didn't know she existed. Didn't she have a right to know who he was? Where she came from?

Her mother didn't know *everything!* Maybe he'd be *happy* to know about Emma.

Now, staring at the picture of Zach Trainer and her mother, Emma knew she had to find out for sure if what she suspected was true.

Turning on her printer, she waited for it to warm up, then printed a copy of the photo.

If it *was* true, if Zach Trainer was her father, she wanted to meet him face-to-face. If it turned out he didn't want to be a part of her life, fine. But at least she would have tried.

This would take some finesse, though. She couldn't just come right out and ask her mother about him.

"I'll have to find out the truth myself," she mur-mured. But how? She gazed out the window of her studio apartment. Although it was the middle of March and spring would officially arrive in less than a week, there was still snow on the ground here in central Ohio, and it was cold.

Emma was sick of winter. She'd been wishing she could afford to go to Mexico or even Florida for her spring break the following week.

She bit her lip, and looked at the Freight Train Web site again. At the top, she saw a link for the year's tour schedule. Clicking on that, she scanned the list to see where the band was now and discovered that the entire month of March they would be in Los Angeles where they were cutting a new album.

The band is reuniting with Jock Livingston, the legendary producer, at Direct Hit, the same studio where they recorded their first multiplatinum album....

Direct Hit Studio.

Her excitement mounted.

It only took her a few seconds to decide that Los Angeles would be a great place to spend her spring break. And with any luck at all, she'd find more than sunshine and warm weather.

Maybe she'd also find a father.

"Thank God for these Wednesday nights!" Zoe Madison declared, sinking onto the nearest chair and grinning at her friends. "Now if only they served booze here at Callie's, life would be perfect."

Shawn McFarland, who was Zoe's best friend, laughed. "Perfect, huh? Can I write that down and remind you later that you said it?"

"Perfect *tonight*," Zoe qualified. "Not perfect, period."

"Oh, I see," Shawn said, elbowing Susan Pickering, another member of their Wednesday night gang, who was sitting next to her.

Susan grimaced. "Personally, I wouldn't mind a drink myself."

"What's wrong?" Zoe asked, forgetting all about her own gripes, which were, after all, just normal.

Susan sighed. "It's same old, same old."

"Sasha?" Shawn asked softly.

Susan nodded.

Every time Susan told them about her younger sister's problems, Zoe counted her blessings. She was so grateful that she'd never had anything serious to worry about with Emma.

"What now?" Shawn probed.

"She got fired from her job at the salon."

"Oh, no," Shawn said.

"Drugs again?" Zoe asked.

Susan nodded. "Maybe, although it could be anything. She stays out too late at night, then can't get up in the morning. Or else she's hungover. Who knows? She says her boss just didn't like her and manufactured an excuse to get rid of her. But that's typical with Sasha. She'll never take responsibility for anything that happens to her. It's always someone else's fault."

Zoe knew someone like that, although she tried not to think about him very often. Not that it was easy when her daughter was a constant reminder.

"She wants to come and stay with me until she finds another job," Susan said.

"You're not going to fall for that again, are you?" Zoe said before she could stop herself. The last time Susan had taken Sasha in, Sasha repaid her by having a party in Susan's house when Susan was out of town on a buying trip, and Sasha's so-called "friends" had trashed the place. Of course, that hadn't been Sasha's fault, either, Zoe thought in disgust.

Zoe saw the look Shawn gave her. Shawn was a lot nicer than Zoe. Zoe had no patience with people who kept letting others walk all over them. On the other hand, Zoe didn't have a sister. It was easy to pass judgement when you'd never walked in the other person's shoes, and she, of all people, should know that.

She made a face. "Susan, I'm sorry. This is none of my business."

"No, it's okay," Susan said. "I feel the same way. I told her no."

"So what's she going to do?" Shawn asked.

Before Susan could answer, Kristie, the owner's daughter and assistant, approached the table to take their order.

Zoe smiled up at the pretty young woman. Kristie was a sweetie. Next to Emma, Zoe considered her to be the coolest kid she knew.

"How's school going?" she asked.

Kristie smiled. "Great."

"How many hours are you taking this semester?" Shawn asked.

"Just nine. I can't manage more and still give Mom the help she needs."

"You're such a good daughter," Shawn said.

Kristie shrugged in embarrassment. "I like working here." Then she grinned. "I get good tips."

"Is that a hint?" Zoe teased.

Now Kristie blushed.

They all laughed.

When they'd settled down, Kristie said, "Are you guys ready to order?"

"Are we?" Zoe asked. "Shouldn't we wait for Ann and Carol?" Ann O'Brien and Carol Carbone, who were sisters, made up the remainder of the Wednesday night group.

Shawn shook her head. "Ann's out of town on business, and Carol has a bad cold."

"Then I guess we're ready," Zoe said.

After Kristie had taken their orders and left the table, Shawn said, "That kid is amazing."

"She is," Susan agreed.

Zoe thought about how Kristie had, without complaint, dropped from being a full-time student at Ohio State to being a part-time student at Tri-City Community College so that she could be here for her mother. Zoe wondered if Emma would have been as generous.

Immediately, she felt guilty. Emma was a wonderful daughter. Except for her ongoing battle to try to find out who her father was, she had never given Zoe a moment's serious worry.

Still, Zoe knew she had spoiled Emma. But what was wrong with that? Emma was her only chick and always would be.

Why *shouldn't* she spoil her?

Maybe if you hadn't been so indulgent, she would have realized how disappointed you are about her going to Pennsylvania for her spring break...

Remembering last night's conversation with Emma, Zoe frowned. The trip to Pennsylvania wasn't the only thing about the conversation that bothered Zoe.

"What's the matter?" Shawn asked.

Zoe made a face. "Are you a mind reader now?"

Shawn smiled. "You're totally transparent, Zoe, at least around us. It doesn't take a mind reader to know something's on your mind."

"It's nothing."

"It must be *something.*"

Zoe shrugged. "Really, it's not a big deal. It's just that Emma's been acting a little weird."

"Emma? Our perfect Emma?" Shawn smiled to show she was teasing. "No, seriously, what's she been doing that you think is weird?"

"I can't really put my finger on what it is. It's odd and hard to explain...it's just that the last couple of days, she's seemed preoccupied and...distant."

Shawn frowned. "How so?"

"I don't know…it's like she's thinking about something else when we talk." Zoe knew she wasn't explaining herself well, yet she couldn't think how else to define the feeling she'd had during the last couple of conversations with her daughter.

"Doesn't she have spring break next week?" Susan asked.

Zoe nodded.

"She's probably just looking forward to it."

"Yeah," Zoe said, "probably." But she wasn't convinced.

"What's she doing for spring break?" Shawn asked.

"Going to Pennsylvania with one of her friends."

"What's in Pennsylvania?" Susan asked.

"Oh, nothing in particular. That's where the friend lives, and Emma said it will be fun just to have a change of scenery." Zoe tried not to show her disappointment over Emma's plans. After all, it was probably totally unrealistic of her to think Emma might want to spend some time with her mother over spring break. Of course she preferred to be with her friends. Hadn't Zoe been the same way when she was young?

Maybe that's what I'm afraid of. That she'll end up being too much like me.

"We have to face it," Shawn said with a sigh. "They all grow up sometime, whether we like it or not."

Zoe knew Shawn was thinking about Lauren, her teenaged daughter.

"Except for Sasha," Susan said wryly.

"So what *is* Sasha going to do now?" Zoe said.

Susan shrugged. "Probably mooch off one of her friends. I'm trying not to care."

"Stay firm," Zoe said.

"I know."

But Zoe wondered if Susan would be able to keep to her decision. Sasha was all the family Susan had, since their father had died in a work-related accident a few months before Sasha was born, and their mother had died of breast cancer when Sasha was eleven and Susan herself was only twenty-five.

Susan'd had a rough time, Zoe thought. She'd practically raised her sister, and it hadn't been easy. Sasha had been rebellious from the very first, almost as if she were punishing Susan for being there instead of their mother. There were times Zoe had wanted to shake Sasha. Other times she wanted to shake Susan.

Still…as she'd said, their relationship was none of her business. But Zoe cared about Susan, and she hated to see her being walked all over by her sister.

Shawn, too, no longer had living parents. They had been killed in an automobile accident less than two years ago. Of course, she now had a wonderful husband, as well as her daughter and a baby on the way.

Zoe was more like Susan. For all intents and purposes, Emma was all the family Zoe had, too. Her parents were still alive, but they had long ago disowned her. She would never forget her father's wrathful shout when she'd left home.

"Once you walk out that door, don't come back!" he'd boomed.

Zoe had looked at her mother, who cowered in the corner. No help there. Her mother was afraid of Zoe's father. Everyone was. The minister of a small church, he had strict religious beliefs and as far as he was concerned, anyone who defied him or questioned his edicts would burn in hell.

Zoe sighed, remembering. She'd never forget the last time she'd called them. It was right after Emma was born. She'd taken a chance, hoping the news that they had a grandchild would soften them and that they might want to see Emma. But her father hadn't even allowed her to tell him about the baby, for he'd hung up on her as soon as he'd realized who it was.

His last words were, "You're dead to us. We have no daughter."

"Zoe?"

"Oh, sorry," Zoe said, blinking at Shawn. "I guess I was daydreaming."

Just then their food came, and the conversation stopped for a while. When it resumed, Susan told them about the new man she was dating, and Shawn talked about the progress of her pregnancy—about which she was ecstatic, because she'd never imagined she'd be able to have another child—and no more was said about Sasha or Emma.

But even though Zoe participated in the lively give-and-take, part of her mind remained on her daughter. She couldn't shake the feeling something was going on with Emma—something she didn't want to share with her mother.

Down deep, Zoe knew Emma's behavior was probably normal. There came a time in every woman's life when she needed to cut the apron strings. To make her own decisions. To begin to take responsibility for her own life.

But even though Zoe understood this, she didn't have to like it.

Emma had never flown into Los Angeles before. As her plane began to lose altitude in preparation for landing, she marveled at the amazing colors below. In Ohio everything was green—or white—depending on the season. But here there was so much brown and gold and ocher. Far from being dull, it was beautiful, she thought. She loved flying through the mountains, seeing them on either side of the plane as it dropped lower.

Now she could see the urban sprawl, the green lawns, the turquoise pools, the pretzel twists of freeways and, beyond, the endless ocean.

There were butterflies in her stomach as the plane banked and made its final approach to LAX—not because of the flight but because of what lay ahead.

Zach Trainer.

She still couldn't believe the world-famous musician might be her father. But no matter how many times she added up what she knew, she came to the same conclusion. Zach Trainer probably *was* her father.

Emma hated that she'd lied to her mother, telling her she was going to Pennsylvania with Jessica for spring break, but it couldn't be helped.

She had to know the truth.

If, as her mother had led her to believe, her father wanted nothing to do with her, so be it. At least Emma would have tried.

Just then there was an announcement telling the flight attendants to be seated for landing. And within minutes, the plane touched the tarmac, then hurtled down the runway. Unconsciously, Emma pushed her foot down as if she were braking a car, then she laughed at herself.

It took thirty minutes to deplane, get to baggage claim and locate her luggage on the carousel. Walking outside, she marveled at the warm weather. Ohio was still suffering from the last vestiges of an extremely cold winter, but here it felt almost like summer. Oh, she could get used to this.

She splurged on a taxi instead of taking a shuttle to her hotel. Why not? she thought. It wasn't every day a girl met her father.

Don't get your hopes up too high. Maybe you're wrong. Maybe he isn't *your father. And even if he is, maybe he'll tell you to take a hike.*

Still, she couldn't banish the anticipation and excitement that had been her constant companion since first seeing the picture that had brought her to this moment.

"First time in L.A.?" asked the driver, glancing at her in the rearview mirror.

"How'd you guess?" Emma said.

"I can spot first-timers a mile away."

Emma grinned.

"So wadda you think of the place?"

"So far I love it."

"Yeah, but you don't live here."

Emma knew he was dying to tell her everything that was wrong with L.A., and since she was feeling generous, she indulged him. He recited all the city's ills—smog, high housing prices, too much traffic, earthquakes, high taxes and too much crime.

"But what about the glorious weather, the mountains, the ocean, Hollywood?" Emma said. "I mean, every city has its problems."

They continued to debate the pros and cons of living in southern California until he pulled up to her hotel. Again, Emma had splurged, choosing a small hotel on Ocean Avenue in Santa Monica. She'd even paid extra for an ocean view. Her mother would have a fit if she knew Emma had increased the limit on her VISA card, but Emma didn't care. What she was doing was an investment in her future. Her emotional future. She'd find a way to pay off the card. After all, she wouldn't be a student forever.

An hour later, she was checked in and had unpacked her one small suitcase. She looked at her watch. It was already four o'clock in the afternoon. Too late to try to see Zach Trainer today.

Besides, it was Saturday. It was debatable whether he'd even be *in* the studio on a Saturday. Seeing Zach Trainer and finding out if he was her father would have to wait until Monday morning.

Telling herself to make the most of what was left of the weekend—to see as much of Los Angeles as she could, starting with Venice Beach, which was nearby—she changed into jeans, a T-shirt and sneakers; tied a hooded fleece jacket around her waist, tucked some cash, her room key and her credit card in her pocket; and headed for the elevators.

Chapter Two

Emma inspected herself in the mirror. She wanted to make a good impression. Otherwise, it might be impossible to get close to Zach Trainer, much less actually talk to him.

And she *had* to talk to him.

She'd thought long and hard about what to wear, finally deciding something conservative and dignified might give her her best shot at gaining admittance to Zach Trainer's inner sanctum. So she'd brought the black dress she'd bought for her last concert performance, and with it she wore black pumps and simple pearl earrings.

Her only other jewelry was her gold watch—her high school graduation gift from her mother—and the emerald birthstone that her mother had given her for her twenty-first birthday.

The weather forecast called for a high of sixty-five degrees, but Emma knew it was likely to be much chillier out this morning, so she added a short, fitted, black-and-white tweed jacket with fringe on the cuffs and lapels to her ensemble.

Satisfied, knowing she looked her best, she took a deep breath.

It was time to go.

When the taxi pulled up in front of an unimpressive, windowless, cinder block building, Emma frowned. "I wanted to go to Direct Hit Studios." She looked at her notebook to check the address she'd given him earlier.

"This is it, girlie." He looked at the meter. "That'll be eight bucks."

Emma couldn't believe it. She'd expected something big and glitzy. This place looked like a glorified pawnshop. But now that she looked closer, she saw the address matched the one she had. Digging into her purse, she pulled out her wallet, extracted a ten dollar bill and handed it to the driver. "Thank you."

"Want me to wait?" the cabbie said.

"I—" Emma considered. She'd started to say no,

but now she changed her mind. What if she couldn't get in? "Would you?"

"Sure."

She knew he didn't expect her to gain admittance, and now that she saw the setup, she wasn't sure she would, either. She'd thought there'd be a lobby and a receptionist. *How naive you are.*

Taking a deep breath, Emma got out of the cab and walked up to the door. She pressed the buzzer next to an intercom-type speaker.

It took a few seconds, but then the speaker crackled to life. "Yes?" It was a female voice.

Emma's stomach was once again filled with butterflies. But she didn't allow her nervousness to show in her voice. "I'm here to see Zach Trainer."

"Name?"

"Emma Madison."

"Do you have an appointment?"

"Um, no, but I—I'm a relative." Emma knew saying this was a gamble, but she was counting on the curiosity of whoever it was on the other end of the intercom. She held her breath.

"Whose relative?"

"Zach Trainer's relative."

"Just a moment, please."

Emma's heart was beating too fast. *Please let me in. Please let me talk to him. Please don't turn me away.*

It seemed to take forever, but finally the voice said, "When the buzzer sounds, you can come in."

Emma turned and flashed a thumbs-up sign to the cabbie, who gave her a salute, then pulled away from the curb.

Emma told herself not to be nervous and took several deep breaths. But she couldn't banish the butterflies. When she opened that door, she'd be walking into an unknown world.

One that might change her life forever.

Sam Welch put his laptop down and walked out of the meeting room where he'd been working and into the studio's reception area. First-time visitors were always surprised at the lack of grandeur. Sam guessed they expected plush carpeting and expensive furnishings.

Instead, two nondescript couches, a battered end table, an equally battered coffee table holding copies of *Rolling Stone, Spin* and *Audiophile* magazines and a seen-better-days receptionist's desk greeted them.

The walls were impressive, though—lined with framed gold and platinum records and CDs as well as signed photos of the musicians and producers who had worked within these walls—Freight Train among them.

Rachel, the receptionist and the one who had called him about the visitor, raised her eyebrows.

Sam nodded, and she pushed the button that would unlock the main door.

Sam was ready to give this caller, whoever she really was, short shrift. Relative. Yeah, right. Just like all the others who'd tried to claim a connection. Sam would've liked to send this one on her way without even seeing her, but what the hell? He'd needed a break, anyway. Might as well hear what she had to say.

Then he could throw her out.

He wondered if this woman was some bimbo Zach had gotten involved with when Sam hadn't been around to keep watch. Unfortunately, his little brother needed a keeper. Sam wondered if Zach would ever grow up. Hell, he was almost forty-three years old! It was certainly time.

Sam ignored the little voice in his head that said *he won't grow up if you keep bailing him out when he gets in trouble...*

Madison.

She'd said her name was Madison.

Sam frowned. The name *did* sound familiar. He was still trying to figure out why when the outside door opened and a young woman walked in. Sam hoped his surprise didn't show on his face, because she was anything but a typical groupie. This was one classy girl.

He took in the creamy skin, the clouds of thick,

curly black hair, the soft gray eyes, the slender yet curvy body, the beautiful face.

A very classy girl.

She was also a very young girl. Sam guessed early twenties. Of course, age had never stopped Zach. When a woman interested him, he didn't care if she was nineteen or forty-nine. He went after her. And so far, Sam had never seen any of those women resist. Such was the lure of fame and money.

Which one of those two was *this* woman interested in? Sam wondered cynically. Stifling a sigh, he walked forward. "Hello. I'm Sam Welch, Freight Train's manager."

"Emma Madison," she said, sticking out her hand.

Something about her smile seemed familiar. He shook her hand, inclined his head and said, "There's a meeting room over there where we can talk."

"Thank you for seeing me," she said once they were inside and seated—her in one of the chairs surrounding the center table, him perched on the edge of the table. She smiled again.

He was determined not to be swayed by her beauty *or* her wide-eyed innocent look. He'd learned a long time ago that a good offense was ten times better than the best defense. "Let's cut to the chase, shall we, Ms. Madison? What's your game?"

For just a moment she seemed taken aback by his

curt question and lack of a return smile, but she quickly recovered.

"I don't have a game," she replied with quiet dignity. "I came here because I have recently come to believe Zach Trainer is my father."

Sam stared at her. He wondered if she had any idea how many times he'd heard similar claims, none of which was ever proven to be true. "You think you're Zach's daughter," he said flatly.

"Yes."

"And why is that?"

Again, she answered quietly. "The year before I was born, my mother was his girlfriend. From what I've been able to find out, she sang with the band and…and they were lovers."

Sam smiled wryly. "That hardly makes her unique."

"Yes, I've read the tabloids. I know he's had a lot of girlfriends over the years."

"You said, *from what I've been able to find out.* What does that mean?"

"Well, the truth is, my mother has never talked about him. In fact, to my knowledge, she's never mentioned his name—to me or to anyone else."

Sam frowned. This was something new. "Who *is* your mother?"

"Her name is Zoe. Zoe Madison." Reaching into her purse, she pulled out a piece of paper and handed it to him. "I printed that picture off the Internet. The girl in the picture is my mother."

As soon as he'd heard her mother's name, Sam was flooded with memories.

Zoe.

That's why the name Madison had sounded familiar to him.

Of course.

Madison had been Zoe's last name.

Beautiful, redheaded Zoe. Zoe of the irresistible smile and adoring gaze, who had only had eyes for Zach. The one girl in Zach's long string of girlfriends who had ever made Sam feel jealous of his younger brother.

Zoe.

Sam could picture her as clearly as if she were there in front of him, instead of her daughter, because he had never forgotten her. He'd only been in her company a couple of times, but she had made a lasting impression.

No wonder this girl looked familiar.

He looked at Emma again. Now that he knew who her mother was, he could see Zoe *in* her daughter. In fact, this girl looked very much like her mother had when she was young.

Except for the color of her hair and eyes, which was what had thrown him off.

Hair and eyes that are the color of Zach's.

Sam wished he could dismiss Emma Madison as

another starstruck groupie or someone looking for a quick buck, but studying her, he knew it was highly possible she was telling the truth.

He gave an internal sigh. "Would you like a Coke or some coffee, Ms. Madison?"

She shook her head. "No, thank you. I'm fine."

Sam looked at her thoughtfully. "So your mother didn't tell you Zach was your father."

"No, she never talked about him."

"Who did you think your father *was?*"

"I've never known what to think. Anytime I asked her any questions, she wouldn't answer. All she ever told me was that she was very young when she got pregnant with me, and that my father didn't know I existed and…if he had, he…he wouldn't have cared."

That sounded like Zach, Sam thought, reminded of all the times Zach had neglected Will, the only child produced from either of his two marriages.

But he knew better than to say so. Although he had a gut feeling she might be right in what she believed, caution and years of experience ruled. There was an enormous amount at stake here, and it was Sam's job to look out for Zach and the band.

So his voice gave nothing away when he said, "Look, Ms. Madison, maybe your mother *was* Zach Trainer's girlfriend for a time, but that doesn't prove a thing. Like I said before, Zach has had hundreds of girlfriends over the years. And believe me, you're not the only one who's tried to shake him down."

He regretted having to say the words, but all the frivolous lawsuits, payoffs and tabloid headlines had made them necessary.

"Shake him down! I'm not trying to shake him down. I don't want money from him. I just want to know my *father!*" Her eyes blazed as they met his.

He forced himself to sound skeptical, even though her passionate response impressed him. "Uh-huh."

"It's the *truth.*"

Sam almost relented when he saw the tears she tried to blink away, but he'd been protecting Zach and his fortune for too long to get careless now. Maybe her story was true; maybe it wasn't.

For now, though, he knew it would be prudent to continue to act as if he didn't believe her, which would give him time to check into her claim. After that…well, he would see….

"Look, Ms. Madison, I agreed to see you because I was curious. I can understand why you might have convinced yourself you're Zach Trainer's daughter, but that doesn't make it true. My advice to you is, go home…wherever your home is…and forget all about this."

The tears still glistened in her eyes, but when she

spoke, her voice was steely. "I didn't come all the way out here from Ohio just to go home with my tail between my legs, Mr. Welch. I intend to stay in Los Angeles until I see Zach Trainer, no matter what you or anyone else says."

Sam shrugged. "It's a free country. And now, Ms. Madison, if you don't mind, I have a lot of work to do." He got up, walked over to the door and opened it.

For a moment, she simply sat there. Then, still not dropping her gaze, she stood, raised her head proudly and, without another word, walked out.

Sam walked back to the engineer's booth. Peering in, he saw the band was taking a break, so he entered the studio. Zach sat perched on a stool. He was talking to Kirby Gates, who had played rhythm guitar with the band for the past three years. Sam liked Kirby, who seemed to have a good head on his shoulders and, unlike many of the other band members, had never caused any trouble or scandal, even though, like Zach, the girls were lined up waiting for him every night.

Zach spotted Sam and lifted his can of Coke in greeting. "Hey, big brother, what's up?" he said when Sam drew closer.

Sam eyed the cigarette in Zach's other hand with distaste. Zach continually ignored the no-smoking convention—another indication of his sense of entitlement. "I need to talk to you for a minute." He looked at Kirby. "Do you mind, Kirby?"

"Certainly not," Kirby said in his upper-crust British accent. "We can punch in that new turnaround later, Zach, okay?"

"Sure," Zach said. He frowned at Sam. "What now?"

"I just had an interesting visitor. I wanted to tell you about her."

Zach's interest picked up visibly. "Her?"

"Yes, *her.* A girl claiming to be your daughter."

Zach grinned and, as always, Sam was struck by his charisma. Trouble was, Sam could see why so many women had fallen for Zach. He was a bad boy. A charming bad boy. Even if he hadn't been a rich, famous musician, he'd probably still be a babe magnet.

"Another daughter, huh?" Zach said. "You sent her packing, right?" He took a long drag on his cigarette, then dropped it into a half-empty soda can.

"Yes, but—" Sam stopped.

Zach raised his eyebrows.

"I think this time the claim might be true."

Zach stared at Sam. Then, getting off the stool, he called out, "Take five, guys. I'll be back." To Sam he said, "Let's go talk outside. I need some air."

Five minutes later, seated in Zach's Hummer, Sam told his brother about Emma Madison's visit.

"I'll be damned," Zach said when Sam had finished. His gray eyes, the exact shade of the girl's, were thoughtful. "Zoe Madison." His smile held memories. "I haven't thought about her in years."

"Is it possible?" Sam asked. "*Could* she be your daughter?"

Zach shrugged. "I guess anything is possible. And you know, I always thought it was weird that Zoe left like that. Hell, she didn't even say goodbye. She just up and left."

"And you never heard from her again?"

"Not a word."

"Did you try to find her?" Sam had never told Zach about seeing Zoe leave that night. He couldn't have said why.

Zach shrugged. "No." He looked at Sam. "Why should I? I figured if she didn't want to be with me, who needed her? Besides, it was probably time to move on, anyway. It was getting a little too serious for me."

Sam was secretly relieved to know it probably wouldn't have made a difference whether he'd told Zach about that night or not.

"So what's she like, this Emma?" Zach said.

Sam hesitated. For some reason, he almost wished he'd never said anything to Zach about Emma Madison. And he knew the reason had nothing to do with protecting his brother. "She's very beautiful," he said reluctantly. "She looks like Zoe, except she has your coloring."

"So you remember Zoe, do you?" Zach's smile was speculative.

"Yes, I remember her."

"And this girl looks like her?"

Sam didn't like the gleam in Zach's eyes. *I shouldn't have told him. Even if he is Emma's father, she's better off without him.* "Yes."

"I want to meet her," Zach said.

"I'm not sure that's a good idea. This could still be a scam."

"Then we'll send her packing."

"I should check her out thoroughly," Sam insisted.

"Fine. Check her out. But in the meantime, I want to meet her. Where is she staying?"

"I don't know."

Zach frowned. "You don't *know?* Why the hell not?"

"Because I didn't ask her."

"Jesus, Sam, I depend on you. You're supposed to be looking out for my interests."

"I am looking out for your interests."

"Then find her for me."

Sam shrugged. "I'll give it a shot, but L.A.'s a big city. It might not be so easy."

"Then hire a private detective. Spend whatever you have to spend. Just find her."

* * *

Emma moped around dejectedly for the rest of the day. But about dinnertime, she got mad. What gave Sam Welch the right to make decisions for his brother? And not even his full brother? He was just Zach's half brother. How could he just dismiss her story like that? Without even *telling* Zach Trainer about her?

How can I talk to Zach Trainer in person? Is there a way?

Her spirits drooped even farther as she realized the futility of what she wanted to do. She probably couldn't get within a mile of Zach Trainer without Sam Welch's approval. Why, Zach probably had a security detail to rival the president's.

I could go to the tabloids. Then he'd have to pay attention to me.

Oh, God. She couldn't believe she had actually had that thought. She couldn't go to the tabloids. She could never do that to her mother.

Totally frustrated and figuring she'd feel a lot better if she got out of the hotel room, she grabbed her fleece jacket, and headed out for a walk. Passing a casual-looking sidewalk café that reminded her of Callie's back home, with its green awning and wrought iron tables and chairs, Emma decided to stop and have some dinner.

Over something called Pecan Crusted Chicken

Salad and iced tea, Emma mulled over the morning's interview once again.

"I should have given him a phone number," she muttered, then looked around in embarrassment. God, she hoped no one had heard her talking to herself.

But why *hadn't* she given him a contact number? After all, he *could* change his mind and decide to further investigate her story.

But even as she told herself this, she slumped back into her chair. Sam Welch wasn't going to call her. He was the protector, the shield between Zach Trainer and everyone who wanted something from him. As long as Sam Welch was around, she would never get anywhere near her father.

She guessed she could hire a lawyer and try to prove her claim in court. But that wasn't what Emma wanted. She wasn't looking for financial support or anything even close. She just wanted the truth.

She wanted a father.

The phone rang right as Zoe sat down to her dinner of a Chicken Fettuccine Lean Cuisine and a salad. Smiling, sure it was Emma, Zoe jumped up and grabbed the portable phone from its cradle. But the caller ID showed the caller to be Shawn, not Emma.

"Hi, Shawn," Zoe said.

"Hi. You busy?"

"Incredibly. You just dragged me away from Lean Cuisine."

"Oh, I'm sorry to interrupt your dinner. Lean Cuisine? What kind of dinner is that?"

"It's the single-working-woman-who's-too-tired-to-cook dinner." Zoe reached for the container of food and took a bite.

"I should let you go, then."

"Don't be silly. As long as you don't mind the sound of chewing while we talk."

Shawn laughed. "Honey, I'm the parent of a teenager. The sound of chewing will be relaxing compared to the noise Lauren can generate."

"How *is* Lauren? I haven't seen her in weeks."

"And whose fault is that? You know you're welcome here anytime. Anyway, Lauren's fine. Really enjoying her junior year." Shawn's voice always softened when she talked about her daughter. "You know, I think she has a boyfriend."

"Oh? Is this a good thing?"

Zoe could almost hear the smile in Shawn's voice. "I think it is. He doesn't live in Maple Hills. He's someone she met at camp. So mostly this romance is carried on via e-mail."

"That *is* a good thing," Zoe said, chuckling. "They can't get into too much trouble electronically. And how about *you?* Are you still having morning sickness?"

"No, thank goodness. It seems to have finally stopped. But there's a downside to that."

"How could there be a downside?"

"Now I seem to be hungry all the time."

Zoe laughed. "Join the club."

"I'm feeling great, though."

"So what's up?" Zoe asked when they'd exhausted the topic of Shawn's pregnancy.

"I wanted to ask for a favor."

"Ask away."

"Would you mind having Trixie for a couple of days next week?"

"Not at all. Trixie's my favorite dog in the world, you know that." Trixie was Lauren's chocolate Lab. "Where are you going?"

"Well, next week is Matt's and Lauren's spring break. Lauren is going to Florida with her buddy Heather and her family, so Matt and I thought we'd spend a few days in New York."

"New York! Why don't you go somewhere *warm?*" Zoe finished off the chicken fettuccine and tossed the container into the trash can.

"Because Matt has never been to New York, and we both think it'll be fun. We're going to try to get some tickets for a Broadway show online before we go."

"If not, just walk down to the TKTS office at Times Square in the afternoon and take your chances."

"That's the half-price place, right?"

"Right. But you need cash. They don't take credit cards."

"Okay, thanks. We might do that."

They talked for a while longer, then Shawn said she had to go. After hanging up, Zoe sat back down at the kitchen table and finished eating her salad.

New York.

So many of her memories centered on the city—memories she'd tried hard to bury. Yet they had never stayed buried. How could they? One of the most momentous things that had ever happened to her had taken place in New York. Sitting there, remembering meeting Zach, she felt suddenly vulnerable.

But that was silly.

As long as she never talked about the past, as long as no one knew what had happened to her and with whom, the past couldn't hurt her.

And yet…the uneasy feeling remained, even after Zoe had gone to bed. For some reason, anytime Emma was away, all Zoe's old fears were resurrected.

Which was totally and completely paranoid, and Zoe knew it. No one in Zoe's life knew anything about her past. No one. Not even Shawn, and Zoe had told Shawn more about her life than anyone in world.

So there was nothing to fear.

Her secret was safe.

* * *

It was after nine before Emma returned to her hotel room. She immediately saw the blinking red light on the phone. She stared, mesmerized and afraid to hope. Who had called? No one knew she was here except Sam Welch.

Her heart pounded as she dialed the number for her messages.

"Ms. Madison?" she heard. "This is Sam Welch. My brother wants to meet you. Can you come down to the studio in the morning? About nine?" He then rattled off a phone number. "Call me back when you get this message."

Emma's hands trembled as she wrote down the phone number. Zach Trainer wanted to meet her!

She took several deep breaths. She didn't want to sound rattled when she called Sam Welch back. She wanted to sound poised and calm.

Finally she felt ready. Picking up the phone, she pressed in the numbers he'd given her.

"Sam Welch."

"H-Hello, Mr. Welch. This is Emma Madison."

"Hello, Emma."

"I—um…nine o'clock tomorrow morning is fine."

"Good. I'll send a car for you at eight-thirty."

"Oh, you don't have to do that. I can take a cab."

"We'll send a car," he said firmly. "The driver will have the front desk call you when he arrives."

"All right. Thank you."

"We'll see you in the morning."

He hung up before she could say goodbye. "Well," she said, staring at the phone still in her hand, "thank you so much, Mr. Welch, you big pain-in-the-butt."

But even her irritation with Zach Trainer's watch-dog who might be her uncle—an uncle she wasn't sure she'd ever feel comfortable around—couldn't dampen her happiness for long. Laughing, she danced around the room like a nut. "I'm going to meet my father, I'm going to meet my father," she sang.

Then, still laughing, she collapsed onto the bed.

Chapter Three

Although she had been giddy and flushed with success and excitement over meeting Zach Trainer the night before, when the time approached to go to the studio the following morning, Emma was scared.

What if she was wrong?

What if everything she believed to be proof that the famous rock musician was her father turned out to be a coincidence?

Could she handle the disappointment?

She wasn't sure, but no matter how filled with anxiety, she knew nothing on earth would keep her from going. She had wanted to know the truth about her father for too long. There was no way she'd pass up this chance.

But she did caution herself against counting on too much. Even though Zach Trainer wanted to see her, and even if he ended up being her father, he still might not want to be a part of her life.

The thought sobered her.

Whatever happens, I'll deal with it....

She was too antsy to wait in her room, so she decided to go down to the lobby of the hotel. Because she'd noticed how casually both Sam and the receptionist at the studio were dressed the day before, today she wore cropped khaki pants and a silk twinset in a deep shade of violet—a color she knew complemented her skin and eyes.

The sweaters had been another gift from her mother. Thinking about her mother made Emma feel guilty again, but she pushed those feelings aside. Time enough for that later, when she had to face Zoe and tell her what she'd been doing this week. Besides, her mother had a lot to answer for herself.

The lobby wasn't busy. It was too early for beachgoers. Only a few early birds were there—a couple of businessmen in suits who were obviously getting together for a breakfast meeting and a young couple drinking coffee and dressed for jogging.

Walking over to the registration desk, Emma told them her name and that she was waiting for a ride.

"We'll let you know when your driver arrives," the model-handsome young man working the desk said. His smile showed perfect teeth. She figured he was an aspiring actor. She'd already seen how many beautiful young people filled service jobs. She felt sorry for them. Acting was an even tougher profession to earn a living at than music, and she knew firsthand how tough *that* was.

She'd seen so many people fail. She still wasn't sure if she wanted to try for a career as a classical pianist. Some days she thought she would enjoy teaching music as much as performing. Other days she wanted to shoot for the stars.

But the statistics for success as a performer were staggeringly low. Still, a huge percentage of success had more to do with grit and sticking to it than it had to do with talent.

And, Emma knew, it also had a lot to do with luck. But she was a firm believer in making your own luck. If you followed up on every opportunity, you had a much better chance of being in the right place at the right time when luck came calling.

Just like I'm doing now, she thought.

Wandering over to the windows overlooking Ocean Avenue, she gazed out. It was overcast this morning, but she knew the fog would burn off within a couple hours. The weather forecast was predicting a sunny, warm day with highs in the low seventies.

By this afternoon, Emma wouldn't need the cardigan part of her twinset.

She'd only been standing there a few minutes when a black SUV with dark tinted windows pulled into the curved drive in front of the hotel and parked in the pickup lane. Not sure if this was her driver or someone else's, she waited where she was. A tall, nice-looking black man dressed in black pants and a form-fitting black T-shirt that showed off sharply defined chest and arm muscles got out and strode into the lobby. He spoke to the registration clerk, who looked her way and signaled.

"Ms. Madison?" the driver said when she reached him. "I'm Bart Johnson, part of Freight Train's security detail."

"Hello," Emma said, sticking out her hand.

He seemed amused, but he took her hand and shook it firmly. "Ready?"

Emma nodded, slung her handbag over her shoulder and walked outside with him.

He opened the back passenger door for her. The leather seats were luxurious, and the vehicle had that new car smell. Emma settled back, telling herself not to be nervous even though she felt a little strange sitting all by herself in the back; left to her own devices she would have gotten in front with him.

Soon they were on their way. Bart Johnson wasn't

a talker like her cab driver had been, but that was okay. Emma didn't feel like making small talk, anyway. He did put a CD in the CD drive, and Emma smiled to realize it was Freight Train's most recent album, *No More Cryin'*.

They'd been driving about ten minutes when she frowned. "Not that I know much about Los Angeles," she said, "but this doesn't seem like the way to the studio."

"We're not going to the studio," he said, making eye contact in the rearview mirror. "We're going to Zach Trainer's house."

"Oh." Zach Trainer's *house?*

"Actually, it's more of a compound," he added. "Off Mulholland Drive. Do you know Mulholland?"

"I've certainly heard of it." Emma had dozens of questions, but she wasn't sure of the propriety of quizzing Bart Johnson about Zach Trainer. Who knew what he'd report to Sam Welch? For she was sure Sam called the shots. As soon as she'd found that photo, she'd immediately researched him and every other person connected to Zach Trainer. And everything she'd learned about the man she believed to be her father indicated he depended on his older brother to handle everything that didn't directly involve creating his music.

Thinking of Sam, she hoped he wouldn't be there this morning. But in another, perverse way, she hoped he was, since at least he was a known quantity. Besides, if Zach Trainer was her father, then Sam Welch was her uncle, and she wanted to get to know him. Who knew? She might actually grow to like him, hard as that was to imagine right now.

Emma took a deep, steadying breath when the car pulled up to an iron gate set in an eight-foot-high brick wall that she assumed surrounded the property.

Bart Johnson pressed a button on the driver's side wall, and a speaker sputtered to life. "It's Bart," he said. "With Ms. Madison."

Seconds later, the gate swung inward, and he drove through.

Wow, Emma thought when she caught her first glimpse of the imposing mansion ahead. She was surprised, too, having imagined that Zach Trainer would live in something starkly modern with lots of glass. Instead, his home was almost antebellum in style—three stories high with a long veranda running the entire width of the front, supported by multiple columns. There were several other buildings of complementary design in the compound, and Emma caught a glimpse of a pool in back as Bart Johnson drove up the winding drive.

Pulling parallel to the shallow front steps, he was out of the truck in a flash and around to her side before she could even think about opening the door herself.

"Thank you," she said, smiling up at him.

"You're welcome," he answered, giving her a little half bow.

Once more, she saw amusement sparking his dark eyes. What had she said that he found so humorous? Wasn't he used to polite people?

Just then, the double front doors opened, framing Sam Welch. Emma had to admit he was kind of sexy—for an older man, that is. He looked strong and fit in his jeans and dark blue shirt. She particularly liked his thick brown hair streaked with gray and the craggy look of his face. His nose was slightly crooked, and she wondered if it had ever been broken. She was curious about his age. She knew Zach was almost forty-three. Since Sam was older, she placed him somewhere in his late forties.

Too bad he wasn't nicer. Didn't he know how to smile? Her insides trembled as she climbed the stairs.

Sam Welch's piercing blue eyes met hers.

And then he surprised her.

He smiled.

The smile changed his face, made him seem softer and friendlier. She found herself returning the smile.

"My brother's back in the studio," he said. "C'mon in, and I'll get him."

"Oh? You have a studio here?"

"Yes, a small one. The band practices there, mostly."

Emma nodded. She would have loved to see it, but even though Sam seemed to have warmed up to her a bit, there was no way she would ask him.

And then he surprised her again. "Want to go with me?"

Emma was on the verge of saying yes when she realized the meeting between her and Zach might be uncomfortable. Maybe it would be best not to have it take place in front of an audience.

"I'll just wait here," she said.

They were standing in a large entryway with a dark, polished wood floor. There were two pale blue velvet chairs on either side of a long refectory table on the left. An enormous arrangement of fresh flowers sat in the middle of the table. Their fragrance perfumed the air.

Across from the table was an arched doorway that led into a formal living room. Emma could see a grand piano at the far end of the room.

Before Emma could sit in one of the chairs, Sam said, "Let's go to the solarium. You'll be more comfortable there."

A studio. A solarium. Emma guessed she wouldn't be surprised to learn there was a ballroom or a bowling alley or a theater. Wow, she thought again.

The solarium turned out to be a huge, glass-domed room at the back of the house that was filled with plants and flowers and casual rattan furniture with yellow-and-white striped seat cushions. Sunlight had begun to break through and the room looked warm and inviting.

Emma sat in one of the large, comfortable chairs. She placed her handbag on the floor. After Sam left to go and get Zach Trainer, she tried to calm her jumpy nerves by taking deep breaths the way she had learned to do before a recital or concert appearance.

What's the worst that can happen? she asked herself. *You'll have to go home without any answers, and you knew that before you came....*

Hearing footsteps, she stiffened, but it wasn't Sam and Zach Trainer entering the room. Instead, a pretty, young, dark-skinned woman with large dark eyes walked in bearing a laden silver tray. She smiled at Emma. "I brought coffee and tea and some croissants," she said in faintly accented English.

Emma smiled back. "Thank you." She was too nervous to eat, even though the croissants and butter and the pot of strawberry jam looked wonderful. She did fix herself a cup of tea. She liked it with cream and sugar instead of lemon. She'd only taken a sip—in fact, the maid was still there—when she heard footsteps again.

She swallowed. *Here we go,* she thought.

Her heart skittered when Zach Trainer entered the room. He looked just like his photos—tall, thin, handsome and cocky. His hair was long and shiny, pulled back with a black leather tie, and he wore skinny black pants and a white, long-sleeved knit shirt.

And his eyes…

They were the eyes she saw when she looked into the mirror. He even had the same thick dark lashes.

No wonder her mother had fallen for him. He was gorgeous.

My father, she thought. *This man, this* icon *is my father.* Her knees felt weak, but this was where her musical training and discipline came to her rescue, for instead of jabbering silly nonsense or falling all over him like a common groupie, she presented the same calm, poised exterior she presented on stage when Sam, stepping forward, said, "Ms. Madison, this is Zach Trainer. Zach, this is Emma Madison."

Emma held out her hand. "Hello, Mr. Trainer."

"Hello, Emma." Smiling, he took her hand, but instead of shaking it, he raised it to his lips and kissed it. "You look so much like your mother. Just as beautiful. Maybe even more beautiful."

Emma's heart pounded. She was mesmerized by him.

"I can't believe I have a daughter," he continued. "But there's no doubt in my mind that you're telling the truth. Hell, all anyone would have to do is look at your eyes to know you belong to me."

"Zach…" There was a warning note in Sam's voice.

Zach gave Emma a conspiratorial wink. "My brother is the sensible one. That's why he takes care of business and I don't."

Emma told herself to guard her heart, but she was already lost to his charm and charisma.

"When were you born, Emma?" Sam asked.

Emma blinked, the spell broken by his question. She told them her birth date. She could see Zach doing the math in his head. His smile was triumphant as he turned to Sam.

"She's mine," he said. "No way she couldn't be. The way I figure it, Zoe was three months pregnant when she left."

Emma's emotions were turbulent. There was the joy of finding her father at last, but there was also a creeping anger at her mother for keeping this moment from her for so long. Why had she done it? What possible reason could she have had?

"Let's sit down," Zach was saying. "I want to know why this is the first I've heard about you."

Emma explained how her mother would never tell her who her father was. "I don't know why," she said when she'd finished.

Zach's smile was wry. "Hey, we were young. I'm sure she figured I wouldn't handle the news well, and the truth is, I probably wouldn't have then." The smile widened. "But none of that really matters, does it? You're here now. That's what counts. And we'll have a blast making up for lost time."

Emma wet her lips. "D-don't you want a DNA test or—"

"What for?" Zach said.

"That's not wise, Zach," Sam interrupted. "DNA testing would protect both of you."

Zach's smile faded as he met his brother's eyes. "I told you. I don't have any doubts about this."

"Ken won't like it."

"Friggin' lawyers," Zach muttered. "They don't like anything."

Emma swallowed. "It would make *me* feel better to have DNA testing done."

Zach looked at her. "You don't have to do this."

"I know, but I want to."

He shrugged. "Okay, fine. Sam, set it up."

Emma glanced at Sam. She saw the slight tightening of his mouth. For the first time, she wondered what it was like for him to work for his younger brother. She was sure there must be friction at times. Yet everything she'd read in the research she'd done about the brothers indicated there was intense loyalty between them. An article in *Rolling Stone* published last year had said, "Sam Welch would walk through fire for his brother, and Zach Trainer seems to feel the same way."

She was really curious about their background. All she knew was that Sam's father had died in a work-related accident when he was three and that his mother, Christine, had married Zach's father eighteen months later. Buster Trainer was an alcoholic, and there were rumors that he had beaten Christine *and* Sam, but neither brother would talk about it. One of the tabloids professed to have interviewed a former neighbor who corroborated the story, but both Sam and Zach had remained closemouthed.

"Now," Zach said, interrupting her thoughts, "where are you staying?"

Emma named her hotel.

"That's too far away." He grinned. "Now that we've found each other, I want you closer. Come and stay here. Tell you what. Why don't you go back and check out? Bart'll drive you and wait for you to pack up your stuff, then he'll bring you back here and you can get settled in. I have to go into the studio this afternoon, but I'll be home by seven. We'll have dinner and we'll talk. How does that sound?"

Emma felt as if she were living in a dream. Maybe she should pinch herself to make sure this was actually happening. "It sounds wonderful."

Zach stood. "Good. Now come here and give your old dad a big hug."

When she felt his arms go around her, Emma's eyes filled with tears. For so long, there had been an empty place in her heart.

But today, like a miracle, that empty place had disappeared.

Sam watched the whole meeting between father and daughter and tried to hold on to his skepticism, but it wasn't easy.

The truth was, Emma was far too appealing.

And even though he wouldn't admit it to Zach, there was no doubt in his mind that her DNA test would show she was Zach's daughter. *And your niece.* Sam swallowed. And his niece.

His emotions were turbulent—part pleasure that this poised, lovely, confident young woman shared their genes and part envy that once again his brother, despite all his screwups, had managed to come out smelling like a rose.

Sam would have given anything to have a son like Will and a daughter like Emma. He only hoped Zach, once he tired of the newness of Emma, wouldn't shunt her aside the way he'd shunted Will.

Thinking about Will, who lived with his mother in Massachusetts, Sam made a mental note to remind Zach to give the boy a call over the weekend. Sam knew the thirteen-year-old lived for his father's phone calls and the increasingly rare visits Zach paid him. Although the custody agreement specified Zach could have his son for a month in the summer, sometimes that hadn't even worked out. It all depended on whether the band was on tour or not. When they were touring, Will's mother—Zach's ex—didn't like the boy to be with them.

Sam understood why. He didn't think it was a good idea for Will to be along on tour, either. The lifestyle wasn't healthy for a kid. Even Zach seemed to realize that.

Sam sighed.

He wondered if Emma was aware of the fact she had a half brother. Surely she must be. The tabloids had written about Will from time to time, even though Laura, Will's mother, had tried to keep him shielded from the limelight as much as possible.

Sam had always liked Laura. His second wife and an intelligent woman, she'd been good for Zach, but Zach had tired of her the same way he eventually tired of all his lovers.

Sam had liked Zoe, too. What was not to like? he thought wryly. She had been enchanting, with a long mop of curly red hair and warm brown eyes and a smile that could melt hearts.

She'd also had a beautiful, rich contralto voice, which is how she and Zach had gotten together. The band had advertised for a female singer, and she'd come to audition. It was a case of lust at first sight, at least on Zach's part. Sam wasn't sure about Zoe. He'd thought she was head over heels for his brother, but after the way she'd just up and left him, maybe in the end that had changed. But while they were together, Sam remembered how he'd felt.

He'd been envious.

Eaten up with envy, in fact.

Just as he was now.

* * *

By Tuesday, when Zoe still hadn't heard from Emma, she decided to call her. She knew Emma hated when she hovered, but Zoe couldn't help it. She missed her daughter. She was used to talking to her several times a week, being a part of her everyday life. And now nearly four days had gone by without hearing from her.

Emma didn't answer her cell phone.

Zoe forced herself to sound casual and lighthearted in her message.

"Hey, it's me. I was just thinking about you and hoping you're having a wonderful time with Jessica. Give me a call when you get a chance."

For the rest of the morning Zoe waited for her cell phone to ring. When it finally did, a few minutes before noon, she snatched it up.

She smiled when she saw Emma's number in the caller ID display. "Hi!"

"Hi, Mom."

"So how's it going? Are you having fun?"

"I'm having a great time. What about you? Working hard?"

Zoe laughed. "I'm always working hard, you know that. But I don't want to talk about me. I want to hear about you and what you're doing. How was your trip there?"

"It was fine."

"Too bad about all the rain."

"Wh—? Oh, yeah. Well, it hasn't bothered us. We met some of Jessica's friends for dinner last night and then we went to a club."

Zoe frowned. What was wrong with Emma? She didn't sound like herself. "Honey, are you *sure* everything's okay?"

"Mom…of course, everything's okay. Quit hovering. I'm twenty-two years old. You don't have to worry about me."

Zoe grimaced. "I know. Sorry."

They continued to talk, with Emma going into great detail about all the things she and Jessica had done and were planning to do the rest of the week, but throughout, Zoe felt there was something Emma wasn't telling her, something Zoe couldn't put her finger on. What that could be, she had no idea.

She told herself she was being silly, doing what Emma had accused her of doing, being a ridiculous worrywart.

And yet…she couldn't shake the feeling that there was something out of sync.

Something Emma didn't want Zoe to know.

Chapter Four

Emma felt terrible after talking to her mother. She knew she should have told Zoe the truth about where she was and what she'd done. But confessing over the phone seemed cowardly. Or was that simply an excuse to put off the inevitable confrontation?

Emma didn't know. She only knew her conscience was bothering her big-time. Yet her guilty feelings didn't diminish her pleasure at being there, in her father's house, which still seemed like a dream.

She had gotten back to the compound shortly after noon, and Bart had insisted on carrying her bags up to her bedroom. Actually, she discovered she'd been given a suite of rooms—bedroom, adjoining sitting room and bath—all private, all gorgeous. The furnishings were elegant, obviously meant for a female guest. The bedroom and sitting room were decorated in shades of rose and white with touches of teal for contrast.

And the bathroom!

Emma nearly swooned with pleasure when she saw the sunken tub and Jacuzzi jets, the thick white towels, the heated towel racks and the array of scented soaps, lotions and oils.

In exploring the suite, she found little touches of luxury everywhere. There were crystal vases filled with fresh flowers in all the rooms. A built-in refrigerator in the bar in the sitting room was stocked with bottles of designer water and soft drinks. A bottle of Australian Shiraz sat on top of the bar, along with a jar of cashews and a bowl of fruit.

Several brand-new books were stacked on the coffee table, as well as the latest issues of *Elle, In Style* and *People.* An Orrefors jar filled with chocolates graced the nightstand in the bedroom. There was a plasma TV and DVD player with a selection of movies, as well as a CD player and dozens of CDs.

It was incredible. Everything a person could possibly want was within reach.

And best of all, the bedroom had a working fireplace *and* a balcony accessible through French doors.

When she opened them and walked outside, she saw her room overlooked the back of the property, with a view of the sparkling pool and the other buildings, and some really spectacular landscaping.

As she gazed down, she saw two gardeners working in the flower beds and a beautiful chocolate Lab sunning himself on the pool decking.

Oh, my, she thought, sighing. *If this isn't heaven, I don't know what is.*

She felt like a princess in a fairy tale. Maybe this really *was* a dream, and in a moment, she'd wake up and be back in her cramped little apartment with its eclectic mix of hand-me-down furniture in still-wintry Ohio.

She'd barely unpacked and put her clothes away when there was a soft knock on the door. Emma opened it to see the same maid who had served her the croissants and tea that morning.

"Ms. Madison," she said, "I just wanted to tell you that your lunch is ready."

As if in answer, Emma's stomach growled. She laughed. "Thanks. I didn't eat much this morning." In a spurt of candor, she added, "Too nervous."

The maid smiled.

Emma had wondered if the servants knew who she was and why she was there. The maid's expression told her they did, and they'd probably been discussing the situation. She wondered what they thought of her. She hoped they didn't think she was after her father's money.

"My name's Emma, by the way. Ms. Madison is way too formal for me. What's your name?"

"I'm Sylvia."

Emma stuck out her hand. "Pleased to meet you, Sylvia."

The maid hesitated, then she shyly took Emma's hand and shook it. "It's nice to meet you, too."

Emma followed Sylvia down the stairs and into a beautiful dining room. When she saw the enormous table, which could easily seat fourteen people, maybe more, and the lone place setting at one end, she made a face. "Can't I eat in the kitchen?"

Sylvia shook her head. "Oh, no. The chef would have a fit. She's very temperamental."

"The *chef*? Mr. Trainer has a *chef*?" She felt odd calling her father Mr. Trainer, but what else could she call him at this point? He hadn't invited her to call him Zach, and she certainly couldn't say *Dad* without being asked. "Exactly how many servants *are* there?"

Sylvia did a silent calculation using her fingers. "Let's see. Not counting the security people, there are eight of us."

"Eight?" Emma couldn't even imagine having *one* servant, let alone eight. "Who are they? What do they do?"

"Well, there's Mrs. Leland, the housekeeper. She

would have come out to meet you, but she's gone to the dentist this afternoon. She supervises the indoor staff. Then there are two of us maids. I'm on the day shift and Kristina—she's from Poland—is on the evening shift. We help in the kitchen and do light cleaning and laundry. Then there's Winnie, the chef, and Marta, who comes twice a week and does the heavy cleaning, and there are two gardeners—Hector and Leon. And then there's Fritz. Fritz takes care of the pool and the cars and he's also Mr. Fixit." She smiled. "He can do just about anything."

There was a note in her voice that made Emma wonder if Fritz occupied a special spot in Sylvia's heart.

"This is a big place to take care of," Sylvia continued.

"I guess." Eight servants. Not counting the security detail. It was enough to make Emma's head spin.

"I'm not sure how many servants Mr. Trainer has in France," Sylvia added.

"France?" Emma said weakly. She guessed she'd read somewhere that her father owned a house in France. On the Riviera somewhere, she believed.

Maybe I'll get to go there sometime.

Even the thought made her insides jump in excitement. More than anything—almost more than she wanted a career in music—Emma wanted to travel. Italy, France, England, Germany, Australia, Russia—she wanted to go everywhere, see everything. She'd never even been to Canada!

As she ate her delicious lunch of warm salmon salad with baby greens accompanied by crusty rolls and topped off with a mouthwatering custard garnished with fresh raspberries, Emma continued to think about the way her father lived, the almost unimaginable extent of his wealth, and how different her life might have been had she been a part of his all these years.

I would have already seen most of those places I've only dreamed about....

And yet...she had had a happy life. Yes, she'd dreamed about traveling when she grew up, but she'd never felt she was missing anything in the way of material things. Her mother had always worked hard and now, as the general manager of Berry's, one of the largest department stores in their area, she was considered a very successful woman. She had certainly given Emma a good life.

All Emma had ever missed out on was knowing her father.

But she knew him now.

Emma only hoped what she had done in contacting Zach wouldn't cause a rift between her and her mother. But if it did, that would be her mother's choice. Because no matter how much Emma loved her mother, she wasn't going to change her mind about this.

She had found her father.

And as long as he was willing, she didn't want to lose him again.

Zoe wished she could get the idea that Emma was keeping something from her out of her mind, but it seemed stuck there permanently. Every time she banished it, it came back.

"Is something wrong?" Bonnie, her secretary, asked later that afternoon.

"Wrong? No. Why?"

Bonnie frowned. "I don't know. You just seem preoccupied, is all."

Zoe almost confided in Bonnie, who had a college-age daughter herself, but stopped herself. She was probably just imagining things. As Shawn had said, Emma was just being normal. Zoe couldn't expect her to share *everything* in her life forever, could she?

Stop worrying. There's nothing wrong.

So why did she still feel uneasy?

Why did she feel as if the other shoe was going to drop any minute?

"Emma, I've been thinking. I want you to stay here in Los Angeles until we have to leave for our new tour at the end of May."

Sam blinked at Zach's pronouncement. His gaze darted to Emma. It was seven-thirty, and the three of them had just sat down to dinner.

"I wish I could," Emma said, the regret in her voice obvious to Sam, "but I'm due back at school next week."

"Really? You're in college?"

"Yes. At Ohio State. I'm a senior. I—" She smiled shyly. "I'm at the School of Music. And I've been accepted into graduate school this fall."

"Music? You're studying *music?*"

"Yes."

Grinning, Zach said, "She's a chip off the old block, Sam."

"Her mother might have had something to do with her musical genes, too," Sam pointed out dryly. "I seem to remember she was a pretty good singer."

"That she was," Zach conceded. He turned back to Emma. "Are you a singer, too?"

"I do some singing, but that's not my main interest. I play the piano, and…I do a little composing." This last was said shyly.

"She *is* a chip off the old block, Sam, no matter what you say!"

Emma blushed.

"After we eat, you have to play for me," Zach continued.

For us, Sam thought.

"For us," Zach corrected, almost as if he'd read Sam's mind. "Something you've written."

"You really want to hear me?"

"Of course I want to hear you."

"I…all right."

For the remainder of the meal, Zach continued to quiz Emma about her life. "What does your mother do?" he finally asked over dessert.

Sam had wondered when he'd get around to Zoe.

"She's the general manager of a big department store in Columbus," Emma said. "Berry's. Have you heard of it?"

Zach shook his head. "I can't picture Zoe doing anything like that."

Emma looked quizzical. "Why not?"

Zach grinned. " 'Cause she was a wild child when she was young."

"Most of us grow up eventually," Sam said.

Zach rolled his eyes. "My brother thinks I'm immature."

Emma glanced at Sam.

Now it was his turn to shrug. "If the shoe fits…"

Zach just laughed. Sam's needling never seemed to bother him. "Lighten up, big brother," was his only comment before he turned his attention back to Emma. "So is your mother married?"

Sam had been wanting to ask the same question.

"No," Emma said.

"Has she ever been?" Zach continued.

Emma shook her head. "No. It's just been the two of us."

That surprised Sam. He'd have thought Zoe was the marrying kind. Certainly she was the kind of girl any man would have wanted to marry. Any man but Zach, he corrected. Marriage had been the last thing on Zach's mind when he was first starting out.

"So let's get back to you, Emma," Zach said. "When will school be out?"

"Not for two more months."

Zach frowned. "Just about the time we'll have to start our world tour."

Sam watched Emma's face. He could see how much she wanted to say she'd stay.

Zach thought for a few more minutes, then snapped his fingers. "I know what. We're starting our tour in London. When school's out, you can join us there! Have you ever been to London?"

"No, I haven't."

Sam heard the longing in her voice.

"Then it's settled," Zach said, grinning. "You'll come to London and travel with us for the summer. You'll love it, Emma. We're booked in London, Paris, Stockholm, Barcelona, Berlin, even Moscow. And then we go to Tokyo, Sydney and Johannesburg. I might have left a few cities out. Sam can give you a complete list."

"I would love to go, but I'm afraid I can't," Emma said.

"What? Why not?"

She sighed. "I have a summer job lined up."

"So? Tell 'em you've had a change in plans."

"I can't. I—" She swallowed. "I need the money."

"Is that all?" Zach said. "You don't have to worry about money anymore. Whatever you need, it's yours. Just give Sam your bank account information, and he'll take care of it." He snapped his fingers. Grinned. "Just like that."

She shook her head. "I can't do that. I—I didn't come here for money."

"I know you didn't, but hell, Emma, I've got more than I can ever spend. And you're my *daughter.* I don't want you working. I want you to spend the summer with me."

"I—" She bit her bottom lip.

"I won't take no for an answer."

Sam saw her waver and knew she'd cave. Ultimately, everyone caved when Zach turned on the charm. But he couldn't blame her. What kid would choose working all summer over an exciting trip to Europe? Still, there was a part of Sam that hoped Emma would be strong enough to keep saying no.

"I *should* say no," she finally said.

"Ah, c'mon, Emma…" Zach said.

Then she laughed. "But I'm not going to. Okay. I'll come to London." Then she jumped up and went around to where Zach sat and hugged him.

Seeing the happiness in her eyes, Sam tried to quash his uneasiness. He wished he could warn her not to count on too much from Zach.

But nothing he could say to Emma would do any good. He knew that from experience. Each person who entered Zach's sphere had to learn his or her lesson the hard way.

All Sam could really do was hope that this time would be different, and that Zach wouldn't disappoint her.

Shyly, yet with secret pride, Emma sat down at the magnificent Steinway grand piano that occupied one corner of the mammoth living room. Normally, she wasn't nervous, since she was accustomed to performing. But this was different. This was for Zach. She wanted him to be proud of her. She breathed a silent prayer her father would approve.

She so wanted him to like "Hidden Places," which was her favorite of the songs she'd composed. This was the first time she'd ever played it for anyone.

In fact, no one knew she wrote popular music, not even her mother. Zoe thought all Emma's leanings were toward classical music, and most of the time, they were.

Pop music was her secret vice, and now she understood why. It was in her genes.

Smiling at Zach, who stood leaning against the fireplace, watching her, she took a deep breath and began to play.

Sam was impressed. Emma was an accomplished pianist and played with passion, confidence and authority.

But it was the sweetness and purity of her voice that touched Sam more than anything else. Sam glanced at Zach. He hoped his brother realized what a special person Emma was, because it was clear to Sam that, even though she'd given in on the summer job, she was the real deal. A remarkable young woman.

Zoe had done a fine job with her.

He thought about what kind of person Emma would be now if she'd grown up in Zach's world. He doubted she'd be anything like this poised, mature young woman.

Zoe had done the right thing in leaving Zach and in keeping Emma a secret all these years.

"That was fantastic!" Zach said. "You're good enough to turn pro."

Sam blinked, realizing that Emma had finished. "Yes," he added, "that was beautiful."

"Thank you," Emma said. Her face was flushed with pride.

"Play another one," Zach said.

So Emma played not just one song, but several more, ending with a classical piece Sam recognized as something famous, although he hadn't a clue as to its title. As the last notes died away, he wondered what Zach was thinking. He was uncharacteristically quiet, seemingly lost in thought.

"Lovely," Sam said. "What was the name of that last piece?"

"Mozart's Piano Concerto Number 1," Emma said. "I played that at a recent concert at the university."

"You're very talented."

Suddenly Zach came to life. "Don't go back to Ohio, Emma. Stay here and practice with us, learn our stuff. Then instead of just coming along on tour, you can be a part of the band. You're good enough to be our lead singer. We'll do some of your songs. And when we do, you can play keyboard, if you like."

"But you already have a lead singer and someone on keyboard," Emma said. She was referring to Daisy Oliver, who was also Zach's current girlfriend, and Todd Bowman, who'd been with the band since the beginning.

Zach shrugged, the way he did anytime someone mentioned a conflict. In his life, all problems had always been conveniently settled with a minimum of disturbance to him. "No big deal," he said. "We'll move Daisy to backup. And Todd, hell, he won't mind an occasional rest."

Sam was chilled by Zach's casual dismissal of Daisy, who was good for him, one of the best choices he'd ever made in a relationship. Sam knew Daisy loved Zach. How could he be so callous toward her? And yet Sam wasn't surprised, not really. Zach was probably right about Todd, though. Todd was confident enough of his own ability that he wouldn't view Emma as a threat. In fact, he'd probably enjoy taking her under his wing and showing her the ropes.

"I wouldn't want to take anyone's place," Emma said. "Even if I *could,* which I can't. Anyway, I have to go back to school."

"If you don't want to sing lead, you can sing backup with the other girls," Zach said, ignoring her comment about school. "C'mon, Emma. What you'll learn by actually performing with the band is worth ten degrees. Hell, what's a degree anyway? Just a piece of paper. I don't have one. And look where I am." His grin was cocky.

"My mother would kill me if I dropped out of school," Emma said, more to herself than to Zach.

"She'll get over it," Zach said.

That night, Sam couldn't sleep. He kept thinking about the stars in Emma's eyes as she lapped up everything Zach had said at dinner and afterwards. He knew it was only a matter of time before she succumbed completely to the lure of Zach's charms and the world he inhabited.

And as much as Sam liked Emma, he knew it would be best for her if she returned to her own life.

The next morning, he woke up early. Once he had his coffee in hand, he got on the Internet and looked up Berry's Department Store in Columbus, Ohio. Within seconds, he had their phone number.

Since it was now nine o'clock in the Eastern time zone and he figured Zoe would already be at work, he picked up his cell phone and thought about what he'd say when he reached her.

"There's a Sam Welch asking to speak with you," Bonnie said. "Do you want to take the call?"

Sam Welch!

The name sent shock waves down Zoe's spine. For a moment, she was too stunned to answer.

"Zoe? Did you hear me?"

Zoe swallowed. "Y-yes, I heard you, Bonnie."

How in the world had Zach's brother found her? And why was he calling?

"Do you want to talk to him?"

No, she didn't want to talk to him. But she was more afraid not to, because Zoe was sure this wasn't a casual call. Not after all these years. Trying to sound calm, Zoe said, "Yes, I'll talk to him."

He can't know about Emma. It's impossible, so there's no reason to be frightened.

Her hands trembled as she waited.

There was a click, then Bonnie said, "Go ahead, Mr. Welch."

"Zoe?"

"Hello, Sam." She was proud of the way her voice didn't reveal any of the turmoil going on inside of her. "This is certainly a surprise. How are you?"

"I'm fine, thank you. And you?"

I was doing great until a few minutes ago. "I can't complain."

"I'm glad to hear it."

Zoe had always appreciated Sam's common sense and loyalty to his brother, but she knew he didn't feel the same way about her. His disapproval had been all too apparent the few times she'd been in his company.

"You're wondering why I'm calling," he said.

"Frankly, yes."

Zoe listened, heart pounding in stunned horror as he told her about Emma showing up at the studio the day before and everything that had transpired since then, including Zach's offer to her of a place in his band.

"I thought you should know," he finished. "Luckily, Emma told us where you worked and what you did."

He wasn't fooling her with his pretended concern. Sam Welch had always been the enforcer in Zach's life, the one who cleaned up Zach's messes and took care of all his problems. Oh, Zoe had read all about Sam. She might not have wanted Emma to know her father, but Zoe had certainly kept herself informed about Zach and his life. There was strength in information.

And that's what Sam was doing now. Cleaning up one of Zach's messes.

Zoe couldn't believe this was happening. She'd been so careful. She hadn't kept anything that would ever tie her to Zach. And yet Emma had discovered the connection. How? How had she found out about Zach? Zoe wanted to ask Sam what she had told them, but she wouldn't give him the satisfaction of showing him how upset she was.

"Say something," Sam said.

"I'm coming out there just as soon as I can book a flight."

"Good. I'll give you my cell phone number. Call me when you know what flight you'll be on, and I'll meet you."

"That's not necessary."

"Same old Zoe, aren't you?"

"What's that supposed to mean?"

"It means you were a spitfire when you were young, and you still are."

Zoe almost smiled. She *had* been a spitfire when she was young. But those days were long gone. Now she thought before she leapt, and she held on to her temper.

"I'll meet you," he said again. "It'll be easier that way."

"Fine."

And then, almost as if he knew what she'd been thinking earlier, he said, "And Zoe?"

"Yes?"

"In case you're wondering, Emma saw a photo of you with Zach on the Internet."

And then he said goodbye.

It only took Bonnie twenty minutes to secure Zoe a seat on a Delta flight leaving the following day and getting to LAX at two-twenty in the afternoon. Zoe would have liked to go immediately, but she knew that was impossible. Even if she could have gotten onto a flight that night, she had too many things she needed to take care of at home and at work before she could leave. This might be the biggest personal crisis she'd ever faced, next to finding out she was pregnant, but that didn't mean the world didn't keep spinning on its axis the same way it always had. Besides, who knew how long she'd be away?

After calling Sam back and giving him her flight information, she thought about calling Emma.

No, that was a bad idea.

Why give Emma any warning? At least this way Zoe would have the element of surprise.

Which might be her *only* advantage.

Chapter Five

Zoe usually brought a book to read in flight, but there was no way she could concentrate on fiction today, not when reality was so fraught with potential disaster.

Damn that photo on the Internet.

Damn it!

After all these years, she would never have believed something so simple would trip her up. Who would have imagined anyone would care about a singer who had briefly had a love affair with a rock star more than twenty years ago?

Oh, God…

If only Emma hadn't seen the photo. And why hadn't she said something to Zoe about it?

Zoe still couldn't believe Emma had gone to California. And lied about where she was going. That was almost as bad as her finding out about Zach. Maybe Zoe was kidding herself, but as far as she knew, this was the first time Emma had ever lied to her. All those elaborate stories about what she and Jessica were doing.

All lies.

But you knew something was wrong, didn't you? She didn't do that *good a job of lying.*

Still…maybe she didn't know her daughter as well as she thought she did. Maybe Emma *had* lied to her before. Maybe she'd lied to her a *lot.*

Oh, now you're being ridiculous. You're just upset and scared because Emma has found out who her father is.

For the first few years after she'd left Zach, Zoe had worried about *him* finding out about *Emma.* But those worries faded as the years passed, especially because—as far as Zoe could tell—he'd made no effort to locate her.

Then when Emma began to question Zoe about her origins, Zoe's worries had changed. Yet she'd never been *really* worried, because she'd honestly believed there was no way Emma would ever find out the truth.

How could she?

Zoe would certainly never tell her. And she'd thrown away anything and everything that could ever connect her to Zach.

Most importantly, even if Emma conducted one of those "find your birth parent" searches, she would find nothing, because there were no records to unearth. Somehow Zoe had had the presence of mind to put *father unknown* on Emma's birth certificate. She'd figured it was better to be slightly embarrassed in front of the nurse taking the information than to have the truth come home to roost sometime in the future.

Yet Emma had discovered the truth.

Zoe closed her eyes.

What am I going to do if she wants to stay with Zach?

Emma was so headstrong and determined when she made up her mind about something. Zoe thought about what Sam had told her. That Zach was trying to persuade Emma to tour with the band instead of returning to school.

The thought was like a knife in Zoe's heart. Emma *couldn't* abandon school. Not after all her hard work. Not when she was so close to graduating and attaining everything she'd ever wanted.

Yes, but that was before she knew who her father was and what he could offer.

Zoe chewed on her lip.

Oh, God. Touring with the band! Zoe thought about

life on the road. The heady freedom. The temptations. The sense that normal rules of behavior didn't apply.

No, I don't want *that for Emma. What am I going to do? Can I count on Sam Welch to help me?*

Zoe wished she knew the real reason behind Sam's phone call. Was he really concerned about Emma? Or did he feel he needed reinforcements to help get Emma away from Zach?

Did it matter?

No. I don't care what *his motives are, just as long as Emma comes home with me.*

Just then the pilot announced their approach to LAX. Zoe tightened her seat belt and gazed out the window.

As the plane headed to its destination, she began to pray.

Sam waited impatiently in baggage claim, which was where he and Zoe had agreed to meet. He wished people meeting arriving passengers were still allowed to go to the gate. Unfortunately, 9/11 had changed the world permanently. Glancing at the arrivals monitor, he saw that Zoe's flight had landed.

Would he recognize her? Did she look anything like the beautiful rebel she'd once been?

He'd never forget the first time he'd seen her.

The band had been performing in Miami—a long gig at one of the beachfront hotels. Sam wasn't working for Zach then; this was years before the band began to achieve the kind of success where they could afford a manager.

Zoe was their lone girl singer, sometimes singing lead, sometimes singing backup when Zach or one of the other guys sang lead.

Sam was still living in Baltimore then, working in the finance department of a bank. He'd taken a week's vacation and had driven down to Miami to see Zach and hear the band. He'd gotten there on Saturday night; the band was already performing.

He'd checked in, then headed for the lounge. He'd first set eyes on Zoe when she walked onto the small stage a few minutes after he'd settled at a table. She was a sight to see. Her wild red curls had tumbled halfway down her back. She'd been dressed in some kind of gold metallic pants and a skimpy little halter top. On someone else the outfit might have looked cheap, but on Zoe, with her fresh, young face, huge brown eyes and incandescent smile, it looked fantastic.

Sam couldn't take his eyes off of her. And when she began to sing in that husky contralto voice, she kept him spellbound. He knew without being told that she and Zach were lovers. Even then, Zach was a babe magnet, the kind of sexy charmer sensible, solid Sam had never been and could never even hope to be.

Later, when the band took a break and Zach spied Sam in the audience, he came down to give Sam a hug and welcome him to Miami. Soon Zoe had joined them. Sam tried not to be envious when Zach put a proprietary arm around her, saying, "Sam, meet Zoe. Zoe, my big brother, Sam."

"It's very nice to meet you," Sam had said. Her hand felt small in his. He didn't want to let it go. Feeling like a fool, he dropped it abruptly, turning away so she wouldn't see the longing in his eyes.

Relationships were difficult for Sam. A former girlfriend had once told him he was too hard to love. "You don't love yourself, that's the problem," she'd said sadly, then moved on to someone else.

Sam knew her accusation was true. He also knew why it was true. When you've been told you're worthless enough times, you start to believe it. But knowing the reason behind something didn't mean you could eliminate the problem.

That trip to Miami had been bittersweet. Sam had enjoyed being with Zach, but he had been uncomfortable around Zoe, and Zoe was always with Zach, so Sam couldn't avoid her. And because he hadn't wanted Zoe or Zach to know the real reason for his discomfort, he pretended to dislike her. In response, she'd been cool to him.

When Zach asked him what his problem was, Sam said he thought it was a mistake for Zach to get mixed up with someone he worked with.

Zach had looked at him as if he had two heads.

"Geez, Sam," he'd said, "you're too damned serious. Lighten up, will you?"

Until the night she left, Sam had been in Zoe's company only one other time, and it was just as uncomfortable, because the attraction he felt for her was as strong as it had been the first time. Maybe even stronger.

And then came Chicago and the night she'd disappeared from Zach's life. Sam had wondered for a long time if there might have been something he could do to prevent her leaving.

Sam had even thought about looking for her, making sure she was all right. But he had no idea where to begin. He knew nothing about her and would have had to quiz Zach, who didn't seem all that upset that she was gone. Zach would have wondered why Sam wanted to find her, would probably even have discouraged Sam. So he'd done nothing and tried to forget her, figuring he'd never see her again.

Yet here he was, all these years later, waiting for her to join him. And he was as nervous as a teenager with his first crush.

Just then a new throng of arriving passengers approached. When the first of them reached the carousel near Sam, he knew she would be there very soon. He scanned the crowd, suddenly spying red hair. He couldn't see the woman; she was hidden from view by a large man.

And then the man moved to his right, and there she was.

Zoe.

He sucked in a breath. She was just as beautiful. Maybe even more beautiful. Because when he'd seen her last, she'd been a girl.

Now she was a woman.

Suddenly, her gaze turned his way. For just a moment, she looked uncertain, then she smiled—that gorgeous smile he'd dreamed of so many times—and raised her hand in greeting.

Dazed, Sam walked forward to meet her.

Zoe would have known Sam anywhere. Except for the smattering of gray hair mixed in with his natural dark brown, he looked exactly the same. His blue eyes were just as piercing, his jaw just as square, his shoulders just as broad, his waist and hips just as trim. All in all, he was a very attractive man.

He also seemed to have mellowed over the years. His smile when he greeted her seemed warm and genuine. She nearly fell over when he kissed her cheek and said he was glad to see her.

Don't be swayed by how attractive he is…or how nice he seems. Zach is the one he cares about. Not you. Not Emma.

"You look wonderful," he said. "I would have known you anywhere."

Zoe couldn't help smiling. "I thought the same thing about you."

"Really? I think I'm a lot different than I was when I was younger."

"I don't see much difference. Not outside, anyway."

"What about these gray hairs?" He grinned.

"They just add character."

He laughed. "That was very diplomatic. So. Did you have a good flight?"

Zoe shrugged. "It was fine. I'm not that crazy about flying."

"I'm not, either."

Zoe spied her bag. "There's my bag."

"I'll get it," Sam said. "Which one?"

Once he'd retrieved her dark green suitcase, he led the way to the parking garage. She raised her eyebrows when she saw his vehicle—a dark green Honda CRV. "What? No sports car? I thought all California moguls drove sports cars."

"I'm hardly a mogul," he said with a crooked smile.

"What are you then?"

"Sometimes I'm not sure myself." He opened the passenger side door and waited until she had buckled herself in before closing it and walking around to the driver's side.

Zoe was still trying to figure out exactly what his cryptic comment had meant when he spoke again.

"Zach doesn't know you're coming."

She turned toward him and their eyes locked. "You didn't tell him?"

"No."

"Why not?"

"I figured you might prefer the element of surprise."

Zoe was taken aback. Could he be telling her the truth? Yes, she *did* prefer the element of surprise, for both Zach *and* Emma, but she wouldn't have imagined Sam would do anything to benefit her at the expense of Zach. Maybe Sam was on her side. Maybe he really did care about Emma's welfare. "I, um, thank you," she finally said.

For the remainder of the ride to Zach's house, they didn't say much. Zoe was too nervous to make small talk, and Sam seemed to understand that. Instead, she looked out the window and marveled at the changes since the last and only time she'd been in the L.A. area.

Everywhere she looked, there was evidence of the explosive population growth. The number of cars on the freeway alone was daunting. Finally they left the freeway and the scenery became more interesting, the vegetation more lush.

As the car wound its way up Mulholland Drive, Zoe said, "How long will the band be in L.A.?"

"Another two months. Then they'll start their world tour."

Zoe swallowed. The tour Zach wanted Emma to join. The tour that must have sounded so much more glamorous and fun than a summer job and going back to school in the fall. The tour Zoe couldn't hope to compete with.

By the time Sam drove his truck through the gates at Zach's home, Zoe had started praying again.

Emma was sitting at the piano, getting ready to practice, when she heard voices coming from the back of the house. At first, she continued flexing her fingers, but suddenly, one of the voices caused her to stop, hands in midair.

Her heart skipped.

Omigod!

Was that her *mother's* voice?

Emma stood, her heart racing. The voices—now she recognized Sam's, too—were getting louder.

That *was* her mother's voice. Emma looked around wildly. There was nowhere to go, nowhere to escape. Not that she would have had time, anyway, because seconds later, her mother and Sam moved into view. They were facing away; neither one saw her standing there.

"I'll just put your suitcase here in the hall for now," Sam was saying. "Why don't you go on into the living room, and I'll see if I can find Emma."

Emma swallowed. She opened her mouth to say

here I am when her mother turned around. Their gazes locked for one long, agonizing moment.

"Mom," Emma said weakly. Her emotions were chaotic. Shame, defiance, love—all warred within.

Sam turned, too. He looked at Emma, then at her mother. He squeezed her mother's arm, said something in a low tone, then walked away.

When her mother entered the living room, Emma didn't know what to say. She knew she should apologize for lying to her mother, but her mother should apologize to her, too. After all, she'd been lying by omission for years. She'd kept Emma from knowing her father!

But it was hard to keep hold of her anger in the face of her mother's obvious concern.

Emma finally moved away from the piano. "I'm sorry, Mom. I should have told you the truth about where I was going."

"Oh, Emma, I'm sorry, too," her mother said.

Seconds later, they were holding each other and hugging tightly.

"Sam called you, didn't he?" Emma said when they broke apart.

"Yes."

"You didn't have to come out here. You could have just called me."

"Oh, Emma, of course I had to come."

"Are you angry?"

Her mother shook her head. "I was at first, but I'm not now." She sighed. "I realize you only did what you felt you had to do."

Emma could feel some of her tension easing. "I'm glad you understand."

"I am concerned, though."

"Why? Everything's fine."

"Is it? Sam told me Zach wants you to drop out of school and tour with the band."

Emma squirmed. "That's not exactly right."

"It's not?"

"No, it's *not*. He doesn't want me to drop out of school. I'd still graduate. I'd…I'd join the tour afterward."

"Doing *what?*"

"Singing. And some playing, too." *Oh, damn. Why did she have to sound so defensive?*

"What about graduate school?"

"I can always go to grad school, Mom. But this tour, it's a once-in-a-lifetime opportunity."

"Opportunity! For *what?* Emma, you're a *classical pianist*. You're not a rock musician."

Emma swallowed. She wished she'd been better prepared for this. Still, there was no time like the present to lay all her cards on the table. "I love rock music," she said with as much dignity as she could muster.

Her mother looked at her as if she'd grown two heads. "Since when?"

"I've always loved it."

"Oh, come on, Emma…"

"Well, I *have*. You know I did my senior thesis on the evolution of rock music."

"But I thought that was an assignment."

"No, the subject was my choice."

"You never told me that."

"You never asked."

"Since when do I have to *ask?*"

"Mom, let's not argue."

"I'm not arguing. I'm just trying to find out how many things you've been hiding from me lately."

Emma sighed. When her mom was like this, there was no talking to her. She could wear you down in no time. "Look, I haven't made any decisions yet. I'm just thinking about the tour, that's all."

"Thinking."

"Yes."

"And if I hadn't come out here, would you have talked to me about it before making a decision?"

Emma wanted to say yes, but something wouldn't allow her to. "I don't know," she answered honestly.

Her mother looked at her for a long moment. Finally she said, "Is Zach here?"

Emma shook her head. "He's in town, at the studio. The band's recording a new album."

"When will he be back?"

"By six or six-thirty. In time for dinner, he said."

"Good."

Emma didn't like the way her mother had said *good.* She had a feeling there would be fireworks tonight. Well, whatever happened, happened. Emma only knew one thing. Going on tour with her father and the band *was* the chance of a lifetime. And nothing her mother could say would change that.

If I decide I want to go, I'm going.

Zoe saw the look on Emma's face and knew the battle was probably already lost. But Zoe was a fighter. She did not give up easily. In fact, she did not give up at all. And she certainly wouldn't now, in what might be considered the biggest challenge of her life.

But for now, she wouldn't press Emma. Time enough for that later, after she'd seen Zach and heard what he had to say. Maybe, if she explained to him exactly what he was asking of Emma, he'd rescind the offer.

"Everything okay in here?"

Zoe turned to see Sam in the doorway. He smiled at her. She smiled back. "We're fine."

"I thought I'd take your bag up to your room."

"Oh, okay."

"Let's go up with him, Mom," Emma said. "I'll ask the maid to bring tea up to my sitting room."

"You have a sitting room?"

Emma grinned. "You probably will, too. This house is unbelievable. There are so many bedrooms and suites, it could be a hotel. It even has a *theater*. A movie theater. Imagine!"

Zoe tried not to let Emma's remarks bother her. So Zach was filthy rich. So what? Emma wasn't the kind of girl to be impressed by money.

Was she?

Oh, God, I can never compete with him.

Upstairs, Zoe discovered Emma had been right. Zoe found herself installed in a small suite consisting of bedroom, sitting room, and bath.

"It's just like mine," Emma said, clearly delighted. "Only the colors are different."

Zoe had wanted to stay in a hotel, but when she found out Emma was staying there, she knew she'd have to swallow her pride. "Maybe Zach won't want me to be here," she said to Sam.

"Oh, he'll want you," Sam said, putting her suitcase down.

Something in his eyes gave Zoe an odd feeling. But she quickly brushed it aside. What was the matter with her? She was reading double meanings into every word out of Sam's mouth.

After making sure she didn't need anything else, Sam left, saying he'd see them at dinner.

Once he'd closed the door behind him, Emma plopped on the bed while Zoe unpacked.

"Mom…"

"What?" Zoe said.

"Tell me about…meeting my father."

Zoe finished putting her lingerie in one of the dresser drawers before turning to face her daughter. The eager, hopeful look in Emma's eyes smote Zoe's heart.

Maybe I was wrong…

She sighed. Walked over to the bed and sat down. Taking Emma's hand in hers, she began to talk.

Chapter Six

"You know I left home the day after I graduated from high school," Zoe said.

Emma nodded. "Yes."

"Well, I went to New York, not Boston."

Emma stared at her.

"I'm sorry, Emma. I've told you a lot of things that weren't exactly true, but only because I wanted to protect you."

"Protect me from *what?*"

Zoe chose her words carefully. "I wanted you to have a normal childhood."

"What's normal about not having a father?" Emma asked bitterly.

Zoe sighed. "I'm sorry, Emma." *God, how many times would she have to say those words?*

"You keep saying that, but I'm not sure you really mean it."

"I really thought I was doing the right thing. Maybe I was wrong. I just don't know. But at the time, I didn't feel as if I had a choice."

"Tell me something, Mom. If you had it to do again, would you change anything?"

"I certainly wouldn't change getting pregnant, because if I did, I wouldn't have you."

"You know that's not what I meant."

"But Emma, the two things go hand in hand. I'm glad I have you, and no, I wouldn't change what I did after I found out I was pregnant, because despite everything, I still believe I did the right thing."

Now it was Emma's turn to sigh. "All right, Mom. I guess we're not going to agree on this, so there's no point in talking about it anymore. Instead, why don't you tell me how you met my father."

"Well, once I got to New York I had to find a job fast because I didn't have a whole lot of money, so I took the first thing I could get, which was working as a cashier in a big music store."

Emma smiled. "So he came into the store?"

"No. Not while I was there, but someone from the band did come in and posted a notice about an audition for girl singers. I saw it, and I decided to go."

Zoe couldn't help smiling at the memory. She'd been so young and so naive. She'd had no idea there would be nearly a hundred hopeful singers there, all with the same goal. Yet somehow, she had stood out from the crowd and Zach had hired her. He'd told her later he'd wanted to hire her the moment he saw her, then when he heard her sing, that clinched it for him.

"So what happened after that?" Emma said.

"Well, the band was playing at a club in the Village at the time, and after a few rehearsals, I started singing with them. I still kept the job at the music store, though. But then about six weeks later they got an offer to play a two-month gig in Atlanta, and I had to choose. I chose the band." Zoe smiled wryly. "Of course, by then Zach and I were...together."

"You were lovers, you mean."

Zoe knew it was ridiculous to be embarrassed. After all, Emma knew they'd been lovers. If they hadn't been, how could she have existed? "Yes, we were lovers."

"Was it love at first sight?"

Zoe heard the wistful note in her daughter's voice. She knew what Emma wanted her to say. But again she had to be honest. There'd been too much subterfuge between them already.

"Emma, we were kids. We didn't know a thing about love. But yes, we were immediately attracted to each other."

That was an understatement. They'd been wild for each other, could hardly keep their hands off each other. Zoe had existed in a state of lust that even now she could remember vividly. But some things were too private to say aloud, even to your daughter.

Maybe *especially* to your daughter.

"How long were you together?"

"Just six months."

"Why did you break up?"

"We didn't. I found out I was pregnant with you and after agonizing over it and weighing all my options, I packed up and left. I didn't even tell Zach I was going." Zoe *did* feel bad about the way she'd left, but again, it had seemed the only way.

Emma was quiet for a long moment. Then, eyes troubled, she said, "Maybe he would have surprised you, Mom. Maybe if you'd told him, he would have wanted you to have me. He might have wanted to be a p-part of my life." Her voice broke at the end, and her eyes filled with tears.

Oh, baby...

Zoe wanted nothing more than to take Emma into her arms. Yet she held back. Now was not the time for sentiment...or fudging of the truth, but she could see the raw emotion in her daughter's eyes, so she knew she had to tread lightly.

"Emma. Sweetheart. I don't want to hurt you, but I don't want you to delude yourself, either. Even if

I had told Zach about you, there was no way the three of us were ever going to be a happy family. Back then, all Zach cared about was making it in the music world. There wasn't room for anything else. And to be fair, I understood that from the beginning. He never made me any promises. Our relationship wasn't like that. I mean, he was only twenty years old. Music was his sole focus."

Zoe stopped, sighed, then plunged on. "And to be completely fair, our relationship was unraveling. I could tell he wanted total freedom, no obligations but his career and the life he was pursuing. If I'd told him I was pregnant, he would have wanted me to have an abortion. I knew if I wanted to keep you, the only way open to me was to leave. And I did want to keep you."

Emma swiped the tears away. "I guess I shouldn't judge you. I know you did what you thought was best. I just wish…I guess I wish you'd given him a chance."

Reaching across the bed, Zoe took Emma's hand. "You know what? Maybe I could have. But from the moment I knew you existed, you were the most important thing in the world to me. I knew I couldn't bear being around anyone who didn't want you just as much as I wanted you." *And that includes my parents.* "I love you, Emma. You know that, don't you? I've only ever wanted the best for you."

Emma reached for a tissue and blotted her eyes. "Of course I know that, Mom. I've never questioned that."

"Then please say you forgive me for keeping this from you."

It seemed to take Emma forever to answer. But she finally nodded, saying softly, "I still wish things had been different…but I forgive you."

Then Zoe did open her arms and, after only a moment's hesitation, Emma leaned forward and allowed herself to be wrapped in Zoe's hug.

After Emma left her mother to unpack, she couldn't settle down to anything. Not even music, which had always soothed her soul when she was troubled. She tried to go back to her practicing but gave up.

Deciding fresh air would make her feel better, she headed outside. The gardeners were working in the front today, trimming the oleanders and bougainvillea, and she nodded to them as she passed by.

It was a beautiful day. Emma took deep breaths of the balmy air. She was so glad to be here. So glad to be out of the winter cold. So glad to have found her father.

What did it matter why her mother had done what she'd done? Wasn't the important thing that Emma was here now? That she and her father had been reunited? That they had a chance to build a relationship?

Everyone made mistakes.

She'd told her mother she forgave her. Shouldn't she live up to those words?

"Hey, gorgeous! Where're you goin'?"

Emma jumped. She hadn't even heard the car coming up the driveway behind her. Zach, grinning at her from an open window, sat in the driver's seat of an enormous black Hummer. Emma could see that another man was in the passenger seat, but she couldn't tell who it was.

"I just wanted some fresh air," she said. "What are you doing home so early?"

"Todd, our keyboardist, has the flu. So I figured, what the hell, and told the guys to knock off for the rest of the day. Anyway, Kirby and me, we're gonna work on a new song this afternoon."

Kirby.

He must mean Kirby Gates, who was the other guitar player in the band. Emma leaned down so she could see in. "Hi," she said. "I'm Emma."

"Hello, Emma."

Emma loved Kirby's upper-crust British accent. And he sure was cute, with longish blond hair and a sexy smile. He reminded her a bit of Jude Law, and she thought Jude Law was just about the sexiest man on the planet.

She tried to remember what she'd read about Kirby. She knew he was young, probably only a couple of years older than she was. She also knew he was single.

And that girls were wild about him, that they followed him everywhere.

She'd seen him do an interview on TV once, and he'd admitted it was hard to find any privacy anywhere.

"It's a pleasure to meet you," he was saying. "Zach's been talking about you for days now."

Emma smiled. "Has he?" Her eyes met her father's, and he winked.

"We're gonna head around back to the studio," Zach said. "We'll see you later, okay?"

"Um, Zach? There's something you should know. My, um, mother is here."

Zach's eyes widened. "Your *mother?* Zoe? Zoe's here?"

"Yes. She arrived a couple of hours ago."

"You called her?"

Emma shook her head. "No, Sam called her. He picked her up at the airport."

Zach frowned. "Why did Sam call her?"

"I don't know." Emma couldn't read Sam. Was he wanting to get rid of her? Or was he worried about her? Or was it her mother Sam was worried about?

Zach's face cleared. "Well, I'll be damned, Zoe." He looked thoughtful. "Kirby, would you mind if we *didn't* work on that song right now? I want to see her mother first. We'll work later."

"You're the boss," Kirby said. Then, smiling at

Emma, he said, "Maybe your beautiful daughter will entertain me in the meantime."

Emma's heart skipped, and she had the oddest feeling as their eyes met. "I'd be happy to," she said.

Sam saw the Hummer as Zach drove past the house. He frowned, wondering why his brother was home so early. He hoped nothing had gone wrong at the studio. Sam should have been there today. Would have been there today if he hadn't gone to the airport. *Damn.*

He watched as Zach parked the truck and he and Kirby Gates climbed out. A few seconds later, Sam saw Emma walk back and join the two men. Sam wondered if Emma had told Zach about Zoe being there.

Well, he'd soon find out.

Because Zach didn't turn toward the studio. He was headed straight for the house.

"Well, well, well, Zoe Madison."

Zoe stared at Zach and willed herself to sound calmer than she felt. "Hello, Zach."

Zach walked forward and put his hands on her shoulders. He looked down at her for a long moment. "You're even more beautiful than the last time I saw you," he murmured, then bent his head to kiss her.

Zoe stiffened, but she allowed the kiss. To turn her head and pull away would have been rude—even unwise—under the circumstances. Especially if she hoped to win Zach over to her side.

"I should be angry with you," he said. "Keeping my daughter away from me all these years." He gave her one of his crooked, sexy smiles—the one that had always gotten him everything he wanted.

"If it had been left up to you, she wouldn't even exist." The minute the words were out of Zoe's mouth, she wanted to take them back.

Instead of being angry, he seemed amused. "C'mon, Zoe, I don't want to fight with you."

"I don't want to fight with you, either, Zach." *I just want to take my daughter far away where she'll be safe. Where you can't hurt her.*

"Then let's call a truce." He gave her another of those smiles. "I want to hear all about what you've been up to the past twenty years." Lowering his voice, he added, "I've missed you."

You haven't changed, Zach. You haven't changed at all. You still think all you have to do is smile and turn on the charm and any woman will just fall at your feet and do whatever it is you want.

"Is that so?" Zoe said with a smile of her own. "I see how hard you tried to find me."

"Now, c'mon, Zoe, be fair. I had no idea where you'd gone."

Besides, Zoe thought, *our romance had just about run its course, hadn't it?* "I'll be fair if you'll be honest. I think you were secretly relieved when I left. Things had gotten a little too heavy for you, hadn't they?"

He opened his mouth to refute what she'd said, then suddenly grinned and shrugged. "You know me too well."

"Yes, I do."

He shrugged again. "Truth is, I probably would've freaked out if I'd known you were pregnant."

Zoe drew a relieved breath. "Thank you, Zach."

But her reprieve didn't last long. Because the next words out of his mouth were, "But now that I know about Emma and have met her, things are different."

Sam cleared his throat, and Zoe gave a start. She'd almost forgotten he was in the room. Briefly, their eyes met, and in his she saw what she imagined was sympathy. Could she trust that? Did he *really* feel sympathetic toward her? Or was she seeing what she wanted to see?

"Emma's a wonderful girl," Zach continued. He grinned. "A chip off the old block, in fact."

"She's nothing like you!" Zoe said before she could stop herself.

"Maybe you don't want to think so, but she sure inherited my musical genes." For the first time since their conversation began, he turned to Sam. "You saw it, too, didn't you, Sam?"

"Zoe's a pretty good musician herself," Sam said.

"So Emma got a double dose of talent." Turning back to her, Zach said, "Zoe, she's great. Good enough that I've asked her to join the band."

"She can't do that," Zoe said. "She's going to graduate school in the fall."

Zach's smile was amused and totally confident. "I think that's for her to decide, don't you?"

Zoe's heart was beating too fast, and she knew why. She was terrified. Of course he was confident. Why shouldn't he be? He'd never known anyone who would turn down the opportunity to be a part of his world.

Zoe only prayed Emma would be different.

Emma and Kirby had decided to sit out by the pool. They hadn't been there five minutes when Sylvia walked out bearing a tray upon which were a plate of cookies and a pitcher of lemonade with two glasses.

"Thanks, Sylvia. That looks wonderful," Emma said.

Once the maid had gone back inside, Kirby said, "So you never knew Zach was your father until recently?"

"No, I didn't."

"Your mum didn't tell you?"

Emma shook her head.

"Why not?"

Emma sighed. She really didn't want to try to explain. Besides, how could she? She didn't understand her mother's reasoning herself. "She says she wanted to protect me."

Kirby slowly nodded. "Zach's lifestyle isn't an ideal way to raise a child," he said thoughtfully. "The truth is, my own parents aren't thrilled that I'm part of the band."

"They're *not?*" Emma couldn't imagine anyone not being proud of Kirby and what he'd accomplished.

"No. They want me to do something more dignified and sensible."

"Like what?"

"You know, banking or law or some other type of business." He smiled.

Emma's heart did a little skip as their eyes met. He was so cute. "Well, I'm glad you didn't."

"I've never been more glad I didn't than at this moment."

Emma swallowed. He was flirting with her. Kirby Gates was flirting with her! "Wh-what do your parents do?" she asked, totally flustered.

"My father is a banker. My mum is a barrister."

"Barrister. That's like a lawyer, right?"

"Exactly like a lawyer." Again, he smiled, and their eyes met.

"But they must have been supportive of your music *sometime* or else how did you ever get to be so good at it?"

"Sure, they were supportive when they thought it

was just a nice hobby. Thing is, no one from the Gates family or the Spencer family—Spencer is my mum's family—has ever done anything so unconventional." He grinned. "My parents have settled down a bit now, though. I think they were worried I was going to get into bad stuff. You know, sex, drugs, rock 'n' roll…"

Emma nodded. She understood. That's what her mother was probably afraid of, too.

"They're probably right about the sex," he said, laughing.

He *was* flirting with her. She could feel herself blushing. "Nothing wrong with that," she said as coolly as she could manage.

He raised his eyebrows. "So if I were to say how about it, you wouldn't say no?"

Emma blushed harder. "I barely know you," she murmured.

"I'm teasing you," he said after a moment. "I can see you're a very well-brought-up girl. In fact, just the kind of girl my mum would heartily approve of."

Emma raised her eyes. *Oh, God. He's gorgeous.* "In other words, I'm boring."

"I didn't say that."

"But you're probably thinking it."

He didn't answer for a long moment. Then, eyes filled with some emotion she couldn't identify, he said softly, "Would you like to know what I'm *really* thinking?"

Emma's heart picked up speed. "I don't know. Would I?"

He reached over and very gently traced a circle on the back of her hand. The most delicious sensation zinged its way up her arm, then flooded her nether regions as their eyes locked.

"I'm thinking you are the most beautiful, most delectable, most desirable girl I've ever seen."

Emma's breath stopped. She couldn't have answered if her life depended on it.

And then, shocking her, but in the nicest possible way, he leaned over and kissed her. At that moment, if Emma had been struck by lightning, she would have died happy. When he drew back, she actually felt a sense of physical loss and it was all she could do to keep from reaching out and bringing his lips back to hers.

"I couldn't resist," he murmured. "You have very kissable lips."

Emma just looked at him. She wished they weren't sitting outside in plain view of anyone passing by. And yet, she almost didn't care. If Kirby had wanted to kiss her again, she would have let him. The way she felt at that moment, if he'd taken all her clothes off and made love to her on the spot, she would have let him. She had a feeling there wasn't anything this man would want from her that she wouldn't be willing to give.

The feeling scared her even as it thrilled her, for she'd never, *ever*, felt this way before.

"Emma?" he said.

She wet her lips. Swallowed. "Yes?"

"I'm not sure what's happening here."

"I—I'm not, either."

"But I want to explore it."

She nodded.

"Is that a yes?"

"That's a yes," she whispered.

"Tonight?"

She nodded again.

"Can you get away?"

"I'll try."

Reaching for her hand, he pulled her up, then led her around the pool to the cabana beyond, only stopping when they were on the other side of the structure, hidden from view by a large cluster of oleander bushes.

Wrapping his arms around her, he bent his head and captured her mouth. Emma's head spun as the kiss went on and on, became two, then three. Finally, he dragged his mouth away. They were both breathing hard.

"I'd better find Zach," he said. His voice was ragged. "Otherwise, I might just have to ravish you now."

Giving her one more fierce kiss, he squeezed her hand, then strode away.

Once he was gone, Emma took several deep breaths until her heart and body calmed. She felt as if she'd taken off in a rocket ship and landed in an unknown world.

And as she slowly made her way back to the house, she knew that nothing in her life would ever be the same again.

Chapter Seven

"I want my two best girls to sit by me," Zach said, standing at the head of the dining room table. "You here, Emma…" He indicated the chair to his right. "And you here, Zoe." He pointed to the place at his left.

Sam gritted his teeth, something he seemed to be doing more and more of lately. *"My two best girls." Zach was such a pain in the ass sometimes! Did he think anyone at this table who had any sense at all was going to believe that line of crap?*

There were times when Sam wanted to deck his brother, and this was one of them. You didn't have to be a rocket scientist to know what Zach was thinking. It was obvious. Zoe was even more desirable now than she had been as a teenager. Sam knew, as certainly as he knew his own name, that Zach would now try to add the grown-up Zoe to the other notches on his belt. He could no more *not* do so than stop breathing.

Sam told himself this was none of his business. If Zoe were stupid enough to fall for Zach's line, then she deserved whatever she got.

But he knew he didn't mean that. He liked Zoe. He didn't want to see her hurt...not again. For no matter what she might say about why she'd left Zach all those years ago, Sam knew it had to have hurt her that she couldn't count on him.

You can't count on him now, either...but you can count on me. The last part of that thought had come unbidden. But Sam knew it was true. Seeing Zoe again had made him realize that she'd always been somewhere in his subconscious, and that he still felt the same way about her. If she ever needed anything, anything at all, Sam would move heaven and earth to get it for her.

But aside from his feelings for Zoe, what about Emma?

She'd be hurt if Zoe was hurt. Sure, she had defied her mother by coming here and seeking out her father, but Sam had seen the love and respect between her and Zoe, even though their relationship was now strained.

You'd think Zach would know better than to make a play for Zoe, but he'd always done whatever he wanted to do with no thought to the consequences.

Zach was like an elephant. He just went wherever he damn well pleased, and if people got trampled in the process, well, that was their problem. The sad thing was, he didn't even realize he *was* trampling them.

Look at him! He was practically salivating over Zoe, even holding her chair out for her. Zach only did that kind of thing when he was homing in for the kill. Sam couldn't stand it another minute.

He walked over and sat next to Zoe, which put Kirby—whom Zach had invited to stay over in the guest house—in the place next to Emma. Sam figured Kirby wouldn't mind. He and Emma would probably enjoy talking to each other, anyway.

"Did you get some rest?" Sam said, turning to face Zoe.

She smiled. "I did, thanks."

When she smiled like that, it made her eyes seem warmer. A man could drown in those eyes. Just looking at her caused his stomach to feel hollow.

Geez, get a grip, Welch. You're not some hormonal teenager, even if you're acting like one.

"Good. Listen, I was thinking. If you'd like to

see some of the sights, I could take you for a drive tomorrow." He looked across at Emma. "You and Emma both."

"Oh, I wouldn't want to impose—"

"It's not an imposition. I'd enjoy showing you around."

"Emma?" Zoe said.

"Hmm?" Emma turned from talking to Kirby.

"Sam has offered to give us a tour tomorrow."

Emma smiled. "That would be nice."

Sam smiled, too, pleased he'd thought of it. "Why don't we plan to leave here around ten? That'll give you two a chance to sleep late."

"Hey," Zach said, "what about me?"

Sam looked at him. "What *about* you?"

"I want to go, too."

"Zach, you've already lost one day of work. I don't think Jock will be too thrilled if you slack off again. Especially since the album is almost finished."

"Screw Jock."

Sam raised his eyebrows. His voice was hard. "Screw Jock? You mean that? When he juggled his schedule to accommodate you?"

Zach looked as if he wanted to say *"Screw you, too,"* but he didn't. "Damn," he muttered instead.

Sam fought the smile that wanted to erupt. *Gotcha.* Turning back to Zoe, he said, "Tell me about Maple Hills. It sounds like a nice town."

"It is. It's wonderful, in fact." She looked across at Emma. "We love it there, don't we, Emma?"

Emma, who had been turned toward Kirby, met her mother's gaze. "I'm sorry, what did you say?"

"I said we love Maple Hills."

Emma nodded. "It *is* nice. It's small, though." She looked at Zach. "You'd probably be bored there, because there's not much to do."

"I like small towns," Kirby said.

"You *do?*" Emma said, turning back to him.

"Very much," he said. "I grew up in one, but we don't call them towns. We call them villages."

"It *was* a nice place to grow up," Emma conceded.

"I'm surprised that you like living in a small town," Zach said to Zoe.

"Why is that?" she said.

"Well, you couldn't wait to leave the small town where you were born." His voice became low and intimate. "Remember how we used to stay up all night in South Beach?"

Sam seethed inwardly.

"That was a long time ago," Zoe said evenly. "I've changed."

"Really?" Now his smile was knowing. "I can't imagine you've changed *that* much."

"That's because you don't know me anymore."

Sam wanted to cheer. But when he looked across the table, he saw how uncomfortable Emma looked, and he felt bad for her. It must be tough to watch your parents spar like this and to know that your mother didn't have much use for your father.

In an effort to diffuse the tension, Sam asked Zoe to tell him about her job.

While she was talking, Sam could see out of the corner of his eye that Zach was frowning. His little brother didn't like not being the center of attention. *Too bad,* he thought. *The entire world doesn't revolve around you, even if you think it does.*

Sometimes Sam wondered how he could love Zach as much as he did, yet not like him much of the time.

While he was mulling over this conundrum, Kristina, the afternoon maid who would serve dinner, walked in carrying two bottles of wine—one red and one white—which she smilingly uncorked, pouring the red into a crystal decanter and plunging the white into an ice bucket. After filling everyone's wineglass with their preference, then pouring large goblets of ice water for each, she left the room.

Zach raised his glass. "To my beautiful daughter and her equally beautiful mother. Welcome to California!"

It would have been churlish for Sam not to join the toast, so he echoed it.

The five of them touched glasses, then drank.

For a long moment, silence reigned. Sam wondered what Zoe was thinking. He knew what Zach was thinking. Then he looked across at Emma. She and Kirby were looking at each other, and something about the expression in their eyes made Sam go still.

Uh-oh, he thought. *This could be trouble.* Under normal circumstances, he'd be happy if these two nice kids were attracted to each other, for Kirby was every bit as appealing as Emma. But these weren't normal circumstances. Emma was already leaning toward abandoning school and hooking up with the band; she didn't need another reason to want to do so.

Poor Zoe. This situation might already be a losing battle for her.

Sam wished there were something he could do to help Zoe, but he'd already done everything he could think of in bringing her out here.

Yet even as he felt bad, even as he couldn't help worrying about Emma—after all, he'd had twenty-plus years of seeing starry-eyed girls who left "real" life to run away with a band, only to end up with broken hearts—something in him knew that the only way he could keep Zoe in his life was if Emma remained a part of it. For wherever Emma was, he knew Zoe wouldn't be far behind.

And the truth was, he'd known yesterday he wanted to keep Zoe in his life.

He wanted that a lot.

* * *

Zoe felt like kissing Sam.

First because he'd offered to give her and Emma some fun time together as well as an opportunity to see some of L.A. And second because he'd thwarted Zach in his bid to come along with them. She'd almost cheered when Zach had had to yield to Sam.

She was beginning to think she'd been wrong about Sam. Maybe he really *did* like her. Or at least not *dislike* her. She glanced at him and found him looking at her. She smiled. His answering smile made her feel good.

With Sam as her ally, maybe things *would* work out. Maybe Emma would realize that in the long run school was more important than the transitory thrill of touring with the band.

Maybe now I can talk to her about my own experience. Not my relationship with Zach, but what it was like on the road. The good things and the bad things. Maybe I can make her understand that it won't all be wonderful the way she imagines it will…that there's a price to pay for everything….

And that sometimes, that price is too high.

But would Emma listen?

Or would she be like Zoe was when she was young and think she knew everything there was to know?

* * *

Emma could hardly wait for dinner to be over. All she could think about was being with Kirby. She hardly tasted the salad, the beef tenderloin, the baby asparagus. Even the crème brûlée, which was one of her favorite things in the world, couldn't compete with the knowledge that soon, very soon, she and Kirby would be alone.

And then...

Her heart sped up just thinking about the possibilities. She knew he was going to want to make love to her, but the thought scared her. It was too soon. She'd just met him.

And yet...Kirby Gates.

Just looking at him made her heart pound harder, her entire body feel weak. She couldn't imagine what she'd feel like if they actually *did* make love....

She shivered. She couldn't let her mind go there or she would give herself away. She had to remember that her mother was watching her. Zach and Sam were watching her, too. And this feeling for Kirby, it was too new and too private. She wasn't ready to share it.

So she tried to concentrate on Zach and what he was saying to her mom.

"I've been thinking about this dilemma of ours, Zoe."

Her mom raised her eyebrows. "What dilemma, Zach?"

Zach smiled. Oh, Emma loved his smile!

"Oh, come on, Zoe, you know…you want Emma to go to graduate school in the fall, and I want her to stay with the band."

"You might join the band?" This came from Kirby, who was clearly delighted at the prospect.

Emma couldn't help smiling back. She nodded. "I'm thinking about it."

"Do you play an instrument?"

"She plays the piano," Zach said. "She's as good as Todd and she sings like an angel."

"You wouldn't know an angel if you fell over one," her mom said.

Emma stared at her mother. Now, why had she said that? She hated that her mother couldn't seem to be civil to her dad. What was *wrong* with her? Emma's gaze darted to Zach. Was he angry?

But he was laughing. He winked at Emma. "Your mother doesn't think much of me, does she?"

"I'm sorry," her mom said. "That was uncalled for."

Zach just shrugged. He was still grinning.

Emma looked at Sam to see his reaction and was startled to see him grinning, too. She guessed she was the only one appalled by her mother's lapse of good manners. But even as she thought this, Emma knew her mother was probably just scared of what Emma's decision was going to be, so she was fighting back the only way she could.

"Anyway," Zach continued, addressing his remarks to her mom again, "I was thinking we might compromise. As soon as we finish recording the album, I thought we might move to a house in your area and stay there until Emma graduates. That way I can see her, but she'll still get her degree. After that, she can come and spend the summer with us on tour, and then, at the end of the summer, if she wants to go back to school, I won't stand in her way." He smiled, obviously pleased with himself. "And if it would make you feel better, you could come along for the summer, too, Zoe."

"I have a job, Zach."

"So? Take a leave."

"I can't just take a leave. I'm the general manager of the store."

"Then quit that job. Hell, I've got enough money for all of us. Don't I, Sam?"

"Leave me out of this, Zach," Sam said.

"Come on, Zoe," Zach said, grinning. "It'll be fun. Just like the old days…"

Emma's mother laughed, but Emma could see she wasn't really amused. "The old days are gone, Zach. They aren't coming back. And neither am I."

Emma wished she could crawl under the table. No one could possibly mistake her mom's meaning.

Zach shrugged. "Okay, so you can't come. But what about Emma? I think my solution is a good one."

Her mother didn't say anything, but she seemed to be thinking.

Emma held her breath. *Please, Mom. Please...*

Just then, her mom looked across the table. Their eyes met and held.

Please...

After a moment, her mother sighed. Then she nodded. "All right. What you've proposed seems fair. And I guess Emma deserves a summer off. She's worked every summer since she turned sixteen." This last was said with pride.

Zach grinned. "Good. Sam, want to get busy finding us a house?"

Emma could hardly contain herself. She knew she was grinning like a fool.

She was going to spend the summer with her father. And almost as good, she was going to tour Europe with Freight Train!

Kirby. I'll be working with Kirby. I'll see him every day and every night....

Would he be as happy about it as she was? *Oh, please be happy, Kirby....*

Turning her gaze to Kirby, she smiled tentatively.

His answering smile told her everything she needed to know.

Zoe couldn't sleep.

The bed was one of the most comfortable she'd

ever had. She had the French doors open to the veranda and the night air was cool and refreshing, and she was certainly tired enough, but her mind refused to shut down. She kept thinking and thinking, not to mention worrying.

Sure, Zach's compromise sounded reasonable and would give her some time to come up with an argument in favor of Emma going to graduate school the way they'd planned, but what if nothing Zoe said or did mattered in the end? What if Emma preferred the life Zach was offering? What if Zoe lost her to his world for good?

I can't bear it. I don't want that life for her. I want her to have the career she's dreamed of. I want her to meet a really nice guy and get married and have babies. I want her to have all the things I didn't have.

And until a few days ago, Zoe had believed this was what Emma wanted, too.

But now…

I can't bear it. I know it's selfish, but I don't want to share her with Zach….

On and on her thoughts whirled.

Finally, Zoe could lie still no longer.

So with the digital clock on her nightstand reading 1:47 a.m., she got up, put on the thick terry cloth robe provided (the one she'd brought was silk and wouldn't protect her against the cool night air), shoved her feet into deerskin moccasins that doubled as slippers and stepped out to the veranda.

It was brighter outside than it had been in her bedroom, for there was a full moon. For a long moment, she stood at the railing and gazed at the silvered grounds. Then, tucking her robe more securely around her, she walked as softly and noiselessly as she could toward the back of the house where she knew there were steps leading from the veranda to the first floor.

She didn't know if there were occupants in the bedrooms she passed, but if there were, she didn't want to disturb them. Just because she couldn't sleep didn't mean others were having the same problem.

She had just reached the stairs when she saw someone walking below. She froze, her heartbeat accelerating. It was a man. He was in the shadows, so she couldn't tell who it was. She knew if he looked up, he'd see her. The white robe would be like a beacon in the moonlight.

Just as he came into full view, he *did* look up. It was Sam. Zoe sucked in a breath, not sure whether to acknowledge him, turn around and pretend she hadn't seen him or do nothing until he passed.

Then the decision was taken away from her, because he stopped and raised his hand in a silent greeting. Later she would wonder why she didn't just raise her hand in reply and wait for him to continue on his way.

Instead, she gripped the stair rail and descended the steps. When she reached the bottom, he walked toward her. "You couldn't sleep either?" he said quietly.

"No," she murmured. "Too revved up, I guess." She was acutely conscious of the fact she wore nothing but a sheer nightgown under her robe, but she assured herself he couldn't see anything.

"Want to talk for a while?" He inclined his head. "We could go sit on the far side of pool. We wouldn't disturb anyone there."

"Sure."

He led the way. Once they were settled in two of the comfortable, cushioned chairs, he said, "I know you're worried about Emma spending the summer with the band."

Zoe sighed. "Yes, I am. I keep thinking I shouldn't have agreed with Zach's plan so readily."

"For what it's worth, I think you were smart to say yes. I think Emma had already made up her mind to go. This way, at least, there's a chance she'll come back home when the summer is over."

"You think?" She wanted to believe this was possible. "Home doesn't have much to offer compared to Zach."

"It has you."

The quiet declaration warmed her and made her see Sam in a whole new way. Had he always been this sensitive? This nice? Had she simply been too young and too wrapped up in Zach to notice before? "Thank you, Sam," she said gratefully.

He smiled. "Don't thank me for stating the obvious." Reaching over, he touched her hand. "Emma's lucky to have a mother like you, and I think she knows it."

Without warning, Zoe's eyes filled with tears. "I hope so."

"Zoe," he said softly, tightening his grip. "She does know it."

Zoe swallowed and nodded. She didn't trust herself to speak.

"She's a great kid. You've done a terrific job with her." He gave her hand a squeeze, then let it go.

Zoe had gotten control of her runaway emotions and was just about to answer when a rustling off to the left startled her. Both she and Sam turned to look. Thinking she'd probably just heard some nocturnal animal in the bushes, Zoe almost laughed at the way she'd jumped when suddenly she spied the shadow of someone slipping past the shrubbery that separated the pool area from the rest of the grounds.

In unspoken agreement, neither she nor Sam moved. Zoe squinted, curious about who else was awake at this hour of the morning.

Then her mouth fell open.

It was Emma.

Emma!

Where on earth had she been? Zoe started to call her daughter's name, but some instinct stopped her. It was apparent, to Zoe, at least, that Emma was moving very stealthily.

And then Zoe saw that Emma wasn't alone.

She tensed, straining to see through the foliage. She'd almost forgotten Sam was there when she felt him move beside her. At that precise moment, Emma giggled. Then, clearly carrying across the yards separating them, a distinctly British voice said, "I'd better leave you here, love."

Zoe's mouth dropped open. It was that guitar player. Kirby. What in the world were they doing together at this time of night? Hadn't he gone to the guest cottage hours ago? Presumably to get some sleep? Zoe clearly remembered him saying he was beat, that if they were going to work the next day, he needed some rest. He'd made a point of saying good-night to everyone.

And now he and Emma were together?

At close to two in the morning?

As these thoughts and more tumbled in her mind, she saw the gap between their two bodies close. Even from here, even with the shield of the shrubbery, it was obvious they were kissing.

And not casually, either.

Zoe was almost ashamed to be watching as Emma and Kirby clung together. She felt like a voyeur and yet she couldn't tear her eyes away.

Zoe realized they must have been together in the guest house. And the way they were kissing told Zoe that although Emma had just met the boy, they might already be sleeping together.

And if they weren't, they soon would be.

Part of her wanted to jump up, run over there and yank Emma away. The other part of her knew that Emma was old enough to make her own decisions, especially about this.

But oh, God, why had she had to meet that boy? It was the worst possible thing that could have happened, because now Zoe knew nothing on the face of the earth would change Emma's mind about the summer.

If there hadn't been reason enough before—with the carrot of spending time with her dad and basking in the attention that would bring from the rest of the world—this new enticement would seal the deal.

The best Zoe could hope for now was that the attraction would run its course. That by the end of the summer Kirby or Emma or both would tire of one another and move on.

As Zoe watched, the two of them broke apart and Emma, laughing softly, waved goodbye and sprinted toward the house. Kirby watched her for a long moment, then turned and soon was lost to sight.

Zoe hadn't realized she been holding her breath until it whooshed out. "Damn," she muttered.

"I was afraid of this," Sam said.

Her head jerked around. "You *knew?*"

"I suspected."

"Why? What happened?"

"Nothing. I just saw the way they looked at each other earlier."

"You mean, at dinner?"

"Yes."

"I must be blind. I didn't notice a thing. I mean, I knew Kirby was being nice to her, but I figured that was because of Zach."

Sam shook his head. "Zoe, Emma's a gorgeous girl. Why *wouldn't* he be nice to her?"

Zoe nodded glumly. "You're right. I was so focused on protecting her from Zach, I forgot I had to worry about lots of other things."

"If it makes you feel any better, Kirby's a nice kid. He's got a good head on his shoulders."

Zoe sighed. "It's just that if she gets tied up with him, that'll be all the more reason she'll want to tour with the band."

"Maybe it's a good thing. Kirby will look out for her."

"I was counting on you to do that."

"I would, but I'm not going with the band this summer."

"You're *not?* I thought as their manager you'd be taking care of all the arrangements."

"I've got two assistants to do that. Truth is, I'm tired of being on the road. I did that for too many years. I've just bought a house, and I'm looking forward to staying put for a while."

Zoe nodded. She understood. She liked being at home best, too. "You have? Where? Here in L.A.?"

"Down in Manhattan Beach."

"But I thought you had an apartment here in Zach's house."

"I'm also tired of living in Zach's houses. I wanted a small place of my own, somewhere I can get away from the music business and the band and everything else."

Yes, Zoe understood that, too. "When will you move in?"

"We're closing next week." He paused. "I almost canceled the deal, though."

"Why? Buyer's remorse?"

"No, not that. It's just that now Zach's talking about selling this place and moving down to Miami. But then I realized it doesn't matter. Our business headquarters can remain in L.A. whether he maintains a residence here or not."

"Why does he want to live in Miami?" Zoe thought about the time they'd played that gig at South Beach, the one Zach had reminded her of tonight. That had been a magical time for her. Before disillusion set in.

"He likes Miami. He saw the place Gloria Estefan has and he's been talking about it ever since." Sam shrugged. "Hell, he could afford to keep this and buy down there, too. He's got enough money to do anything he wants to do—as he pointed out at dinner." This last was said dryly.

"Does it bother you that he's done so well?"

"No, not really. I never wanted that kind of fame *or* money. Thing is, people are always wanting a piece of Zach, whereas I can live the way I want to. Privately. Besides, I have all the money I need."

Zoe nodded. She relished her uncomplicated life. She couldn't imagine being followed around by paparazzi, your every move chronicled for the world to see, never having a moment of peace unless you were behind a fence. Emma didn't understand what that kind of life was like, that there was a big price to pay for fame and fortune.

"The only thing that bothers me," Sam said thoughtfully, "is when Zach tries to use his money to bribe people to do what *he* wants them to do."

"Like he did with me tonight."

"Exactly. By the way, I'm glad you refused him."

Zoe smiled. "There wasn't anything he could have said that would have induced me to agree to take a penny of his money."

Sam sat thinking for a long moment. Then he said softly, "Tell me something, Zoe."

"What?"

"Why didn't you tell Zach about Emma? Why did you just leave?"

"Lots of reasons. But the main one was, I knew he wouldn't want me to have her. And even though I was scared, I wanted her."

Sam nodded. "And afterward? Why didn't you ask for child support?"

"Because I wanted her to have a different kind of life than she would have had if people had known about her." She sighed again. "But now that's all changed. When word gets out about Emma, nothing will ever be the same."

"That's true, but you've given her a solid foundation, Zoe. I think she'll be able to handle the other stuff now."

"Once she gets over being mad at me."

Sam smiled. "I think she's over it already."

They talked a few more minutes, then Zoe yawned.

"You ready to go back inside?"

"Yeah, I think maybe I can sleep now." Zoe wasn't sure why she felt better. Nothing had been solved, plus now she had one more thing to worry about with the discovery of Emma's and Kirby's involvement. Maybe it was Sam's steadying presence that had helped her. Or maybe it was that she'd finally realized she couldn't control what Emma did. The only person's actions she could control were her own.

Sam walked her to the foot of the stairs leading up to the veranda. "You still think you'll feel like sightseeing later?"

"Sure, I still want to go. What about you? If you want to change your mind, it's okay."

"I don't want to change my mind. But we can leave later, if you like."

"No, ten o'clock is fine."

"Okay. I'll see you at breakfast then."

"All right." She gave him a grateful smile. "Thanks, Sam."

"What for?"

"For being a friend."

"You sound surprised."

"I guess I am. I confess I always thought you didn't like me."

He regarded her silently for a moment. "The truth is," he finally said, "I've always liked you too much." And then he leaned over and brushed his lips against her cheek. "Sweet dreams, Zoe."

Before she could answer, he turned around and walked away.

Chapter Eight

What the hell are you playing at? Sam asked himself as he climbed into bed. *You know there's no way you can have a relationship with Zoe. You're Zach's brother, and the last thing on earth she'd want is to get involved with anyone in Zach's family.*

On that sobering thought, Sam punched up his pillow and closed his eyes.

But he kept thinking of how she'd looked tonight. So soft and feminine. So vulnerable. He knew she had a successful career, that she was capable and more than able of taking care of herself. Hell, hadn't she raised Emma on her own? Didn't that show she didn't need anyone's help?

And yet, looking at her tonight, hearing the uncertainty and worry in her voice, all he'd wanted was to put his arms around her and tell her she wasn't alone.

This is crazy, you know. You're setting yourself up for a fall. There's no way she'll want to get involved with you. Not on any level. So it's a damn good thing she's leaving in a couple of days....

When he finally fell asleep, he dreamed of her. In his dream, she was the young Zoe. The girl who had so enchanted him. The girl he'd wanted for his own.

In the dream, she came to him, and they made love. It was so real, Sam moaned in his sleep.

The next morning, when he awoke to sunlight streaming into his bedroom, he knew he had to be careful. Otherwise he was in danger of ending up with a badly bruised heart. In fact, if he were smart, he'd stay as far away from Zoe as he could.

If you were really smart, you'd go downstairs and make some kind of excuse, tell her and Emma you can't take them sightseeing today, that something important has come up and you have to go into the office.

And then you'd run like hell.

Zoe set her alarm for nine o'clock, but she woke up before eight. Her eyes felt grainy from lack of sleep, and her head was pounding. Hopefully, some Advil and a shower would make her feel human again.

Forty minutes later, she'd downed the Advil, showered, washed and dried her hair and had dressed casually in black pants and a short-sleeved russet sweater. Ready to face the others, she headed toward the stairs.

Thinking it might be a good idea to make sure Emma was awake, Zoe stopped in front of her daughter's bedroom door and knocked softly. After a few seconds, she knocked harder. When she still hadn't been acknowledged, she tried the knob and found the door open. A quick glance inside told her the bedroom was empty. Maybe Emma was in the shower.

But the bathroom and adjoining sitting room were also empty. Emma must already be downstairs.

Good, Zoe thought. They wouldn't keep Sam waiting.

When Zoe entered the dining room, Zach, Kirby and Emma were just getting up from the table. Judging from the dirty dishes sitting there, they'd already had their breakfast.

"Oh, hi, Mom," Emma said, smiling. She looked fresh and lovely with no traces of her late night, and had already dressed for the day in low-rider jeans, clogs, white T-shirt and a body-hugging, short pink jacket.

Zach's smile and glance was admiring as he looked Zoe up and down. "Good morning, Zoe. Did you have a comfortable night?" He lifted a black jacket from the back of his chair and put it on.

"Yes, thank you, I did." The last thing she wanted was for Zach to know how disturbed she'd been last night.

Kirby also smiled at her and added his good morning to the others.

Zoe wanted to dislike him, but she couldn't. He really *did* seem like a nice kid. If he was someone who lived in their area and had a normal profession, she would have been happy for Emma.

She said her good mornings, then turned to Emma. "We're not leaving until ten, honey. Sit and talk to me while I have my breakfast?"

"Well, actually," Emma said, "I was going to write you a note. I, um, I'm not going with you today."

"Why not?"

Emma glanced at Zach. "Zach invited me to come and watch the band record today, and I didn't figure you'd mind if I went to the studio instead of with you guys. I mean, I can sightsee anytime, but I won't get another opportunity to watch Jock Livingston work."

"But Emma, I was looking forward to spending today with you. And you're going to be with the band all summer."

"I know, but—" Emma looked uncomfortable.

"Hey, no problem," Zach said. "Why don't you come to the studio with us, too, Zoe? You'd probably enjoy seeing the way things have changed over the years. And that way you and Emma can still have the day together."

Zoe almost said yes. Then she thought about Sam. She couldn't do that to him. Not after he'd been so nice to her. Not after the way he'd stuck up for her.

Not after what he said...

"Thank you, but I believe I'll stick with my original plan." She glanced at Emma, hoping her daughter would change her mind.

But Emma just smiled apologetically.

Damn. I'd like to kill Zach.

"We'll see you at dinner, then," Zach said. He smiled at Emma. "Ready?"

"I just need to run up and get my handbag," she said. Walking over to Zoe, she gave her a hug. "'Bye, Mom. See you later. Have fun."

"You, too," Zoe said. She gave Zach a dirty look, but he pretended not to see it.

Minutes later, they were gone.

Zoe fumed after they left. She was so frustrated. How could she ever win against Zach? He had everything going for him. Money. Fame. An exciting life.

This morning was a perfect example of how he could undermine anything Zoe had to offer. Emma must have known when Zach had asked her if she wanted to go to the studio instead of sightseeing how much Zoe was looking forward to spending the day with her. It had been obvious last night when they'd planned the excursion. Yet the moment her father suggested something more attractive, Emma had had no qualms about disappointing her mother.

Of course, Zoe thought ruefully, the inducement of spending the day in Kirby's company had probably had more than a little to do with Emma's desertion.

Zoe sighed. She might as well go home tomorrow. There was obviously no reason to stay on until Sunday, when she assumed Emma would be going back. Staying longer would just make her feel more impotent than she did already.

Besides, the longer she stayed, the more chance she'd say something to Emma that would make things worse. Zoe knew herself too well. Sometimes, no matter how she tried, she said things that would be better left unsaid. And then she suffered the consequences.

I can't afford to do that with Emma. Not now.

"Good morning."

Zoe jumped. She'd been so lost in her thoughts, she hadn't heard anyone enter the room. "Hello," she said to the older, pleasant-looking woman who stood there.

"I'm Mrs. Leland, the housekeeper."

Walking forward, Zoe stuck out her hand. "Hello. I'm Zoe Madison, Emma's mother."

The Leland woman seemed taken aback, but she finally took Zoe's hand and shook it. "Yes, they told me you were here."

Zoe could just imagine what the servants had had to say about the situation.

Mrs. Leland began to clear the soiled dishes from the table. "I don't normally do this but Sylvia, our daytime maid, called in sick this morning." She rolled her eyes. "What would you like for breakfast? Eggs and bacon? An omelette? Pancakes? Winnie—that's our chef—will make anything you want."

"Right now, I'd just love some coffee. And then maybe some fruit and wheat toast?"

The housekeeper smiled. "All right. I'll just take these dishes out to the kitchen and come right back with that coffee."

Good as her word, she returned in minutes with a glass carafe of steaming coffee and a small jug of cream. After filling Zoe's cup, she said, "Winnie says we've got fresh strawberries, grapefruit, melon or all three. And for your toast, there's strawberry and raspberry jam."

"Strawberries and melon sound wonderful, and I'll have the raspberry jam."

"Me, too, Mrs. Leland. But I also want scrambled eggs and bacon."

Zoe turned at the sound of Sam's voice. "Good morning." He looked great. Why was it men didn't show a lack of sleep the way women seemed to? He even looked younger today, too, in jeans paired with a blue sweater the exact shade of his eyes.

Zoe wondered if he realized how attractive he was. *Of course he does. A man in his position earning the kind of money he must earn probably has admiring women lined up in droves....*

"Good morning." He walked over and sat across from her. After studying her a moment, he frowned. "What's wrong?"

Zoe made a face. "You know, I have a friend back home who can read my moods just like you seem to be doing." She heaved a sigh. "It's no big deal, I guess, but Emma's not coming with us this morning."

"Why not?"

"She had a more attractive offer."

"Don't tell me. Let me guess. Zach invited her to go to the studio with him."

"How'd you know?"

Sam's smile was wry. "Think about it, Zoe. In his shoes, isn't that what *you'd* have done?"

Zoe drank some of her coffee while she considered his question. "So what you're saying is, he'll use every tool at his disposal to turn her head."

"Again, in his shoes, wouldn't you?"

She nodded glumly.

"I'm only surprised he didn't invite you to come along."

Zoe hesitated. Their eyes met across the table.

"So he *did* invite you?"

"Yes," she admitted.

"Why didn't you go?"

"I—" She stopped. It would sound egotistical to tell Sam she hadn't want to disappoint him. "The truth is, spending the day with you sounded a lot more pleasant than sitting in a dark studio all day long."

"You're not a very good liar, Zoe."

"Why do you think I'm lying?"

"Because I know you'd prefer to keep an eye on Emma. No matter what else was offered."

"You really *can* read my mind. Okay. The reason I didn't go with them was it didn't feel right. I don't want Emma to think I don't trust her."

"Whatever the reason, I'm glad you didn't change your mind."

His tone and the expression in his eyes made Zoe's heart flutter. Boy, she was pathetic. It had been so long since a man had indicated he found her attractive—at least a man she found attractive, too—that she didn't know how to act.

Just then Mrs. Leland walked in with a laden tray. After that, they busied themselves with their food and the subject of Emma and Zach and the studio was dropped. But Zoe knew, no matter how much she enjoyed the day with Sam—and she was sure she *would* enjoy it—she wouldn't be able to banish the problem of Emma from her mind.

How could she?

She and Zach were battling for Emma's heart, and at the moment, he seemed to be holding the winning hand.

The moment Sam saw Zoe that morning, he knew he was doomed. There was no way he was going to turn tail and run, much less forget about her. No way. She'd stolen into his heart a long time ago, and pretending he could just stop caring about her was ridiculous.

Face it, Sam old boy.

You're hooked.

Sitting across the table from her, just the two of them, he couldn't help thinking how nice it would be to have this to look forward to every morning.

Okay, if that's the case, go for it. Figure out how to make her forget you're Zach's brother. Figure out how to win her for yourself.

But that was easier said than done. First there were some logistics to figure out. Like how to eliminate the thousands of miles between where she lived and where he lived. Because how could he work on winning her if he was here and she was in Ohio?

Suddenly he had a disturbing thought. What if she already *had* someone in her life? What then?

He watched as she spread jam over a slice of toast. She was so beautiful. He wondered what she'd say if she knew what he was thinking. He wanted to ask her if she was involved with anyone, but he couldn't just blurt it out.

At that moment, she looked up and saw him studying her.

"What?" she said, smiling quizzically.

"I was just thinking how beautiful you are."

Color stained her cheeks and her gaze slid away. "I'm not."

"Why are you embarrassed?" he said softly. "I'm just stating the obvious."

She put the piece of toast down. "I'm embarrassed because I'm not used to compliments like that."

"No one's told you you're beautiful before?"

"Not for a long time."

"Are you telling me there are no men in your life?"

She smiled wryly. "That's what I'm saying."

Sam wanted to jump up and cheer. "The men in Ohio must be blind. Either that or stupid."

Now she really *did* blush.

Sam lowered his voice. *Go for it.* "We'll have to change that, Zoe. We'll have to change that starting now."

"Ready for some lunch?"

Zoe looked at her watch. It was after two. She smiled at Sam. "I *am* a little hungry."

"I know the perfect place. It's on Ocean Boulevard—they've got terrific seafood, and if you like, we can sit outside."

"Sounds great."

It had been a wonderful day so far. They'd walked on the beach, driven high up into the Hollywood hills where they'd had terrific views of the city, and Sam had driven her through some of the tonier neighborhoods where she'd enjoyed seeing the beautiful homes and lush landscaping. They'd even found a parking place right off Rodeo Drive and spent an hour ambling along the posh street looking into the windows of the expensive shops.

Zoe enjoyed taking mental notes and had even gotten some ideas to take back to work with her.

The weather had cooperated, too. The temperature was a balmy sixty-seven, and the sun had been shining all day. A nice change from home, Zoe thought.

All throughout, she was acutely aware of him, of how attractive he was, and the things he had said to her last night and this morning kept humming through her mind.

Sam, she kept thinking. *Sam Welch.* Who would have imagined she would feel this way about him? And in such a short time?

I'm as bad as Emma. I certainly have no right to judge her over Kirby, because the truth is, if Sam wanted to make love to me this afternoon, I would probably let him....

And it wasn't because she was sex starved, either, no matter *what* her women friends thought. She grinned. Well, maybe she *was* sex starved, but she had standards. She wouldn't jump in the sack with just any good-looking, sexy guy. No, it was *this* good-looking, sexy guy she wanted. And miraculously, he seemed to feel the same way.

"Here we are," Sam said, breaking into her thoughts. He pulled into the parking lot of a medium-sized restaurant boasting a large outdoor eating area covered by a blue-and-white striped awning and encircled by a white fence over which deep purple and scarlet bougainvillea grew rampant. They were close to the Santa Monica Pier and its famous carousel. In fact, when they got out of the car, Zoe could hear the faint sound of the music from the carousel, although most of it was drowned out by the powerful surf and the squawks of the ever-present seagulls.

Zoe took a deep, satisfied breath. Although she wouldn't have traded Maple Hills for anything, she had to admit if you could afford to live in southern California—especially if you could afford to be close to the ocean—it would be mighty tempting to do so.

Sam held the door open, and Zoe walked inside. The restaurant was only about half-full, the lunch crowd mostly gone. A young, beautiful hostess dressed in black approached with a smile showing perfect teeth. Aspiring actress, Zoe thought.

"Two for lunch?" she asked.

"Yes," Sam said. "And we'd like a table outside."

"Certainly." Picking up two menus from the hostess station, she said, "Follow me, please," and led them out another door that opened directly into the outdoor dining area. Indicating a table that afforded an excellent view of the ocean, she waited until they were seated, then handed each a menu. "Your waiter will be with you in a moment," she said. "Enjoy your meal."

"Gorgeous girl," Zoe said when the hostess walked away.

"They're all gorgeous out here," Sam said. "They all want to be movie stars."

Zoe nodded. Poor kids. Most of them didn't stand a chance of succeeding, no matter how beautiful and talented they were. And yet…who was she to feel sorry for them? They were chasing their dreams. Didn't everyone have the right to chase their dreams?

"I recommend the scallops or the yellowfin tuna," Sam said. "Both are specialities of the restaurant."

"I love scallops," Zoe said, her mouth already watering just thinking of them.

By the time their waiter—another gorgeous young person, only this time a male—arrived, they'd already made up their minds about what they wanted and were ready to order.

Once the waiter had gone off to place their orders—Zoe had ordered the scallops and Sam the tuna—Sam said, "I've been thinking."

"Uh-oh, that sounds ominous."

He grinned. "Zach wants me to find a place near Maple Hills for him to live until the band goes on tour."

"Yes, he said that last night."

His eyes met hers. "What would you think about me finding a small place for myself?"

Zoe's heart skipped. "You mean, in Maple Hills?"

"Yes."

"Why would you do that?"

"You know why," he said softly.

"No, I don't."

"Because I don't want to say goodbye to you. I've thought about you for years, Zoe. My brother was a moron for letting you go, but I'm not. I think you and I have something going on between us, something that could turn out to be important, and I want a chance to see if it will work."

She loved his eyes. They were so blue. So direct. So honest.

"Well? What do you say?"

"I—" She toyed with her cutlery to give her time to think. The trouble was, she was so out of practice. She hadn't had a relationship in a long time. "I do feel the way you do," she finally said. "And I'd love for you to come to Maple Hills. But—"

"But what?"

"Well, we seem to have a few strikes against us."

He grinned. "Only a few?"

She couldn't help laughing.

His smile faded. "I'm willing to take a chance, Zoe. Are you?"

Was she? The last time she'd jumped without a safety net, she'd ended up pregnant and alone. Heart beating a little too fast, she took a deep breath and nodded. "Maybe. Yes, I think I am." As soon as she'd said the words, she felt elated. Maybe she was crazy. Maybe she'd end up getting hurt. Maybe, with so many things against them, there was no way they could ever sustain a relationship. But if you were always worried about the "what ifs" you'd never do anything.

A few seconds later, their food arrived, and while they ate, they didn't talk. They simply enjoyed their food and the beautiful view. But every so often, their eyes would meet, and Zoe would feel warm straight down to her toes.

The last thing she'd ever imagined when she'd boarded that plane yesterday was that a little more than twenty-four hours later she'd be sitting across from Sam Welch and contemplating taking him as a lover.

And yet here she was.

And except for the situation with Emma, she felt happier and more excited than she'd felt in a long time.

Chapter Nine

"Damn."

"What?" Zoe said, alarmed.

Then she saw them. Half a dozen vans, trucks and cars parked along the road outside the gate to Zach's house. The vans had call letters on the sides. Oh, God. They belonged to reporters from TV and radio stations. Some of them might even be from the tabloids.

As Sam's SUV drew closer, doors opened and closed, disgorging men and women with cameras.

"Why are they here?" Zoe asked.

Sam's jaw tightened. "I don't know. But I can guess."

Zoe swallowed. "You mean…Emma?"

He nodded. "Afraid so."

"But how do they know about her?"

Sam shrugged. "Someone leaked something. Probably one of the servants. Or maybe someone from the studio."

"C-can we just ignore them?"

"In a situation like this, I've learned it's best to just bite the bullet and answer their questions as briefly as possible. Otherwise, they'll speculate and write all kinds of stuff that isn't true."

Zoe took a deep, steadying breath.

He glanced over at her. "You okay?"

"I'm fine."

"Okay. Here we go, then." Sam pulled up to the gate and stopped the truck. "Ready?"

"As I'll ever be," Zoe muttered.

He smiled at her, then rolled down the windows.

The reporters, all talking at once, rushed forward.

"Sam!"

"Sam!"

"Mr. Welch, is it true that Zach Trainer has a grown daughter and that she's out here in L.A. now?"

"Can you tell us if the rumor about Zach Trainer's daughter is true? Is she here?"

"Who's her mother? Did Zach know about her before now? Where's she been hiding?"

They continued to shout questions at Sam as cameras whirred and hand mikes were thrust at his face.

He held up his hands. "Slow down. One at a time. You, there." He pointed at a skinny young man who looked as if he were still in high school. "Your name's what, Jeff?"

The young man grinned. "That's right. Jeff Brightwell, KCBS TV. Is it true that Zach Trainer has recently discovered he has a grown daughter?"

"Yes, it's true," Sam said.

The crowd erupted with more questions.

Again, Sam held up his hand. "You're next." He pointed to a pretty blonde in a red dress.

"Hi, Mr. Welch. I'm Gina O'Malley from KNBC TV. What's Zach's daughter's name? And where's she been hiding all these years?"

"Her name is Emma, and she hasn't been hiding. She lives in Ohio."

"Emma what?" the blond said.

Sam looked at Zoe. "They'll find out sometime," he said *sotto voce.*

Zoe sighed and nodded.

"Emma Madison," Sam said.

"Mr. Welch! Mr. Welch!" A very pretty dark-haired girl waved wildly.

"Yes?" Sam said.

"How old is Emma?"

"Twenty-two," Zoe muttered.

"Twenty-two," Sam said.

"Who's her mother?"

"Her mother is a woman Zach knew in the early days. Before the band was famous. You wouldn't know her."

"But what's her *name?*" the man named Jeff asked.

Zoe sighed again. "They'll find out anyway," she said softly. "You might as well tell them."

"Her name is Zoe Madison," Sam said. "Now, if you don't mind, I'd like to pull into the grounds."

"One more question, Sam?" This came from an older man whose eyes were hidden by dark glasses.

"Yes, Bob?" Sam said.

"How does Zach feel about this newly discovered daughter of his?"

"You'll have to ask him about that," Sam said with a smile.

"Ah, come on, Sam," the reporter said, "you're not fooling us. You know everything there is to know about your brother. Why don't you just tell us?"

Sam reached over and squeezed Zoe's hand.

"It's okay," she murmured.

"The truth is, he's thrilled to have found Emma. I'm sure he'll be giving you a statement soon."

And with that, he reached over and pressed the button on the speaker, then quickly identified himself. Seconds later, the gates swung open.

Zoe didn't breathe easily until they'd closed behind them.

"You okay?" he asked as he drove to the back of the house, out of sight of the reporters.

"Yeah, I'm okay." But she was shaken. Now the whole world would know about her and Zach. About Emma. Oh, God. Everyone in Maple Hills would know! And the people at work. What would they think? What would they say? Would she ever have a moment of privacy again?

Shawn, she thought.

I have to call Shawn. I don't want her to read about this in the paper or hear about it on television. And I'd better call right away.

"This is just the beginning," Sam warned as they walked into the house.

"I know. Listen, I have to make some phone calls. I'm going up to my suite."

"All right." He smiled down at her. "Don't look so worried, Zoe. They'll get tired of this story soon enough."

"I hope you're right."

Five minutes later, Zoe sat on the sofa in her sitting room and placed a call to Shawn.

The call was answered on the second ring. "Stella Vogle's office."

"Shawn?"

"Zoe? Where *are* you? I called your office today and Bonnie said you'd taken off for Los Angeles."

"Yes, that's where I am. I should have called you, I know, but, well, there were extenuating circumstances."

"You sound upset. What's going on?"

"It's a very long story, but I'll have to give you the short version."

"Okay."

"What happened is, Emma discovered the identity of her father and she came out here to L.A. to try to see him instead of going to Pennsylvania on her spring break."

"Oh, my."

Zoe knew Shawn was dying to ask the obvious question. "Anyway, as soon as I found out what she'd done, I got on the next plane to practice some damage control."

"That sounds ominous."

Zoe took a deep breath. "The thing is, Emma's father is Zach Trainer."

"Zach Trainer? *The* Zach Trainer?"

"One and the same."

"Omigod," Shawn said. "Zoe! I'm stunned."

"Yeah, so was Emma."

"I hardly know what to say. Did…did anyone else know about this?"

"No. Only me."

"Not even *him?*"

"Not even him."

"Omigod," Shawn said again. "How did you meet him?"

"I'm going to have to tell you the whole story when I get back, which, by the way, will be soon. I haven't made my return reservation yet, but I'll probably come home tomorrow. Or maybe Saturday. I'll let you know. Anyway, very short version is, I went to New York after graduating from high school, worked in a music store, saw a notice about a band needing a girl singer, auditioned and got the job. The band was Freight Train, before they made it big. Zach and I became lovers. I got pregnant. I knew he didn't want any commitments and would want me to have an abortion, so I took off. He didn't know anything about Emma, and that's the way I wanted it."

"Oh, Zoe. No wonder you never talked about him. How did Emma find out?"

"She saw a picture on the Internet. Of me with him. She put two and two together." Zoe grimaced. "As luck would have it, the band is recording a new album right now, so she was able to locate him easily. I'm not sure how she talked her way into seeing him, but you know Emma. Once she sets her mind to something…"

Shawn chuckled. "Kind of like her mother that way, isn't she?"

Zoe smiled, but the smile quickly faded. "Anyway, I knew I needed to call you and let you know what was going on because today the media got hold of the story. They were camping out by the entrance to Zach's house awhile ago. For all I know, they're still there waiting for him to come home."

"Wait a minute. You mean you're *staying* at Zach Trainer's house?"

"I hadn't planned to, but Emma was here, so I thought it was probably a good idea for me to be here, too."

"Wow," Shawn said.

"The whole story will probably hit the news tonight. Before it does, I was hoping you could call Susan and Carol and Ann…and even Callie…and let them know what to expect."

"Of course I will."

"I still have to call Bonnie and warn her. You never know. Reporters might show up at the store."

"Oh, poor Zoe. Your life won't be your own from now on."

"Tell me about it," Zoe said grimly.

"How's Emma doing?"

"Oh, she's in seventh heaven. Just floating around like Cinderella." Zoe hadn't meant to sound bitter, yet she knew she did. "Oh, hell, I don't blame her. She's thrilled. Not only has she found her father, but he's famous and rich and has welcomed her with open arms."

"It would be hard not to be thrilled."

"Yeah, I know. And Shawn, the worst thing is, he wants her to join the band."

"What?"

"Yeah, that was *my* reaction."

"But how can she? She has school."

"She's planning to come home and finish this year out. But she probably won't be going to graduate school."

"Oh, Zoe, that's too bad. And yet…"

"I know. It's a huge opportunity for her."

"Yes, it is."

"In her shoes, I'd probably want to do the same thing," Zoe finally admitted. "The band's scheduled to tour Europe starting in June."

"Wow."

"Yeah. Wow."

For a moment, they were both silent. Then Zoe said, "Enough about me. How're you feeling?"

"Kind of puny right now. My feet are swelling something awful."

"Did you call the doctor?"

"Yes. She's prescribed a diuretic and said I should drink lots of water and keep my feet elevated as much as possible."

"That's kind of hard when you're still working."

"Stella's offered me a leave starting now, but gee, I hate to do that to her. Bad enough I was planning to take three months off after the baby's born."

Zoe knew Shawn wished she could be a stay-at-home mom once the baby was born, but Matt, her husband, didn't make a whole lot of money as a teacher, and with Lauren looking at college in another year plus having a baby to raise, they would need Shawn's salary.

They talked a few minutes more, then Zoe said she'd better go so she could get Bonnie before some local reporter figured out where Zoe worked and called the store.

Half an hour later, exhausted from having to tell an abbreviated version of her life story twice in the past hour, Zoe left her suite and headed downstairs to look for Sam.

She found him in the sunroom. He was talking on a cell phone and doing something on his laptop at the same time. She cleared her throat so he'd know she was there.

When he turned and spotted her, his face lit up. Seeing it, Zoe's heart melted. She couldn't remember the last time a man she cared about had looked at her in just that way. Maybe no one ever had. Certainly Zach never had. Yes, they'd been mad for each other's bodies, but there hadn't been the kind of connection she'd seen between couples like Shawn and Matt, for instance.

The kind of connection I want. The kind of connection I might be able to have with Sam, if we're lucky.

Concluding his conversation, Sam said, "I just talked to Zach. Told him about the reporters waiting for him."

"Are they still there?"

"Yep. They won't leave till they talk to him."

Zoe sighed. She seemed to be doing a lot of sighing lately. "I thought maybe they'd lose interest after you talked to them."

Sam smiled cynically. "They'll want every last drop of blood, and if they don't get it, they'll dig until they find it. Or worse, they'll make up things. A couple of those people out there were from the tabloids. The ones I ignored."

Zoe groaned. She thought about the horrible headlines she'd read on some of those papers in the supermarket checkout lanes. The ones that said things like Serena Starlet Marries An Alien and Frankie Famous Actor Admits Fathering More Than Sixteen Children.

"Zach said if they're still out there when he comes home, he'll invite them onto the grounds and have an impromptu press conference. Introduce them to Emma."

"Oh, Sam, is that necessary?"

"I'm afraid it is, Zoe. Better that he does it now. Maybe he can diffuse the gossip if he shows that he doesn't think what's happened is out of the ordinary." His eyes were full of sympathy. "I know you hate this, but it was inevitable. Face it. Emma's life is no longer her own. Yours won't be for a while, either."

"For a while? You mean there's hope they'll eventually get tired of me?"

He grinned. "You'll have your fifteen minutes of fame, then they'll move on to someone else."

"I hope you're right." Belatedly, Zoe thought about her parents. Oh, God. The press would have a field day when they discovered she'd left home and had never been back. And when they found out—as she was sure they would!—that her father was an extremely conservative fundamentalist preacher who had disowned her, they'd go nuts. And as much as her father's attitude had hurt her, she still didn't want to see him or her mother spread across the tabloids.

Sam frowned. "What else is bothering you, Zoe?"

She made a face. "You have to stop doing that."

"Doing what?"

"Reading my mind."

He smiled. "It's not hard, you know. Your face is an open book."

"I was just thinking about my parents. This will be bad if the press gets wind of their existence."

"Because…?"

"Because they're very private people. My father is a minister of an extremely conservative church. The fact is, when I left home, he told me not to come back."

Sam's face hardened. "And he's a *minister?* I thought men of God were supposed to be compassionate."

"Compassionate is not a word I'd use to describe my father. He lives by a rigid code of conduct, and he expects his family and congregation to live the same way. And when they don't, he denounces them."

Sam looked at her for a long moment. "Did you ever go home again?"

"No. I called my mother when I found out I was pregnant, but my father wouldn't talk to me. He told my mother to tell me he no longer had a daughter."

"Jesus. I'm sorry, Zoe."

"Yes, me, too. It doesn't hurt anymore, and I know you probably think he doesn't deserve my pity, but I know what this kind of publicity would do to him, Sam. It would ruin him. He wouldn't be able to hold his head up in his church again. And I don't want that for him. Yes, I think he was wrong in the way he treated me, but he is what he is. And I don't want him to have his entire life torn apart because of me and what I've done."

"You're a better person than I am, then, because in your shoes, I'd be thinking the hell with him."

"He's my father, Sam. Right or wrong, he's still my father."

Sam didn't say anything for a long moment.

Then, quietly, he said, "I don't remember my father." His eyes met hers. "He died when I was two."

"What happened? Was he sick?"

"No. He worked in a manufacturing plant. There was a malfunction in one of the big pieces of machinery. It started a fire, and my father didn't get out."

"Oh, Sam. That's awful."

"Yeah, my mother was pretty torn up. Scared, too. She'd never been on her own." He grimaced. "A year later, she met Buster Trainer and married him. Zach's father. Buster the Bastard is what I call him." His voice was hard.

Zoe had read the rumors about Zach's father. "I take it this wasn't a happy marriage."

Sam's laugh was ugly. "No, it wasn't happy. It's my theory he married our mother more for the settlement money she got when my dad was killed than anything else. And I think she realized her mistake early on, but she kept making excuses for him. Thing is, Buster liked his liquor, and when he was liquored up, he liked to use his fists. Women, kids, it was all the same to him." He pointed to his nose. "The reason my nose is crooked is I finally fought back. He put me in the hospital. The good thing to come out of that is our mother finally got up the courage to leave him."

"She's no longer alive, is she?"

"No. She died of breast cancer a year and a half ago."

"That's what I thought. There was an article in the paper about it. What about him? Zach's father?"

"He died years ago. Motorcycle accident." Sam smiled cynically. "But not before squeezing as much money as possible out of Zach."

No wonder Zach had never talked about his father. Zoe didn't blame him. Knowing about Buster helped her understand why Sam had always been so protective of Zach. It also helped her better understand Zach's determination to be a success.

Just then, Sam's cell phone rang. Zoe walked over to the windows and gazed out at the beautiful grounds while Sam talked. A few minutes later, she heard him end the call.

"Zach and Emma are on their way," he said.

Zoe turned.

"He wants us to join them when he talks to the reporters."

Zoe nodded. "Okay."

"Don't look so grim. Zach's an old hand at this. You won't have to say much."

But Zach was used to dealing with the media. Zoe, on the other hand, felt like a prime filet mignon about to be set before a pack of hungry wolves.

Chapter Ten

If Emma hadn't already made up her mind to join the band once she graduated, today would have clinched the deal for her. It had been such a *fabulous* day. She felt exhilarated after watching the band work. She'd always known that reading about something or seeing it in the movies or on TV was a poor substitute for actually experiencing it firsthand.

Today had certainly proved that. Watching the guys work, especially watching Jock Livingston work *with* them, was a revelation to her.

Cutting an album was a far cry from performing at a concert. And as much as Emma loved classical music, she found the energy and passion exhibited by the band members to be an incredible high.

But the most thrilling thing of all had been when Zach had asked her if she wanted to try singing back-up with Daisy on the last song they'd recorded. It was easy to learn. She pretty much had the part nailed after she'd heard them rehearse it twice.

At first she'd been afraid Daisy might resent her, but the singer was friendly and helpful. Emma breathed a sigh of relief. The last thing she wanted was to cause any kind of friction between Zach and Daisy; for she could see that Daisy was in love with Zach.

Emma imagined lots of women had been in love with him over the years. She wanted to resent the fact he took the adulation for granted, but how could she?

Of course he took it for granted. He was famous, rich, handsome. He'd been conditioned to expect nothing less than worship.

I'm just as bad as any of those women, she thought. *I adore him, too. And so did my mother once upon a time.*

She sure didn't adore him now, though.

Emma sighed. She wished her mother would get over her negative feelings about Zach. Sure, she knew some of those feelings might be justified, but good grief, that was all water under the bridge now.

What had happened between them had happened twenty-three years ago. It was time to get over it. Because Zach was now a part of Emma's life, and that made him a part of her mother's life, too. And Emma wanted everyone to get along. They didn't have to *love* each other; Emma knew that wasn't going to happen. But she didn't think it was asking too much for them to be courteous to one another, even friendly.

I have to talk to Mom. Maybe once she realizes how important this is to me, she'll try harder....

Glancing at Zach, Emma saw that he was deep in thought. The two of them were now on their way home. Today Bart was doing the driving, so Emma and Zach were sitting side by side in the back.

Emma knew there were reporters waiting for them at the house. Zach had told her about Sam's call and that soon everyone in the world would know about her and her relationship to him.

Emma didn't mind. She was proud to be Zach's daughter, and she didn't care who knew it. She wondered if that's what had Zach so quiet, if he was thinking about the upcoming confrontation.

The thought had barely crystalized when he turned to her with a smile. "Emma, I've been thinking about something."

She smiled back. "I could tell."

"When I talk to the reporters, I'd like to tell them

that you're going to change your name and from now on you'll be known as Emma Trainer."

Emma blinked, stunned by what he'd just said. Change her name? She tried it out in her mind.

Emma Trainer.

"You mean officially change it?"

"Yes, officially. You're my daughter. I want you to have my name."

Emma thought about how Liv Tyler had changed her name after she found out she wasn't Todd Rundgren's daughter but had instead been fathered by Steven Tyler.

This wasn't *so* different, was it?

Emma swallowed. *Emma Trainer.* Oh, she wanted to have Zach's name. She wanted to really badly. And yet…wouldn't her mother be hurt if she did this? Wouldn't it make things even worse between them?

I can't do this…no matter how much I want to, I can't unless I talk to Mom about it first….

"I'm so honored that you'd ask me," she finally said, "And I wish I could, but I just can't."

"Why not?"

"I'm afraid my mom's feelings would be really hurt. I have to talk to her about it first. I—I hope you understand."

"You know, Emma, your mother has had you to herself, name and all, for twenty-two years. I don't think it's wrong for me to want my turn. Do you?"

When he put it that way, what could she say? After all, he was right. "No, I don't. But—"

"Then it's settled," he said with a smile.

She shook her head. "Zach…let me talk to my mother first. I—"

"Look, Emma, it only makes sense for you to take my name. Especially now that you're going to be part of the band. Don't worry about it, okay? I have an idea that I think she'll like." He smiled and reached for her hand. "There's one more thing. I'd also really like it if you called me Dad."

Overwhelmed by emotion, Emma's eyes filled with tears. "I—I would love that…Dad," she answered softly.

Leaning over, he kissed her cheek. Emma gave him a tremulous smile. Her heart felt so full. In her wildest dreams of finding her father, she had never imagined anything like this. "I—I've been wanting to ask you something, too."

"Okay."

"I know I have a half brother…."

"Will," he said.

"I—I'd really like to meet him."

"Would you?"

"Yes."

"He lives in Massachusetts, you know."

"Yes, I know."

"Okay. Well, maybe after I come to Ohio, we can

fly up and see him over a weekend. Or he can come to Ohio."

Emma smiled. "That would be great." After a moment, she added, "You don't see much of Will, do you?"

Her dad shrugged. "His mother prefers to have him out of the limelight, and I have to respect that."

Emma nodded. That was what her own mother had wanted, too. Emma wondered how Will felt about spending so little time with his dad. Did he wish things were different the way she had?

"What's he like?" she asked.

"Will? He's a nice kid. Kind of quiet."

"Is he interested in music, too?"

"No, not at all. He takes after his mother more than he does me."

"What *does* interest him?"

"He likes to read…and draw."

Emma smiled. "So he *is* creative."

"Yeah, I guess so."

Emma wished her father didn't sound so distant when he talked about Will. It made her uncomfortable and a little sad that he didn't seem to have much interest in her half brother. It also made her wonder if he might eventually lose interest in *her,* too.

She quickly banished the thought. Of course he wouldn't. He probably was just one of those people who didn't relate to younger children and who liked them better when they were adults. There were lots of people like that. It didn't mean they didn't *love* their children.

"Will is what?" she asked. "Thirteen?"

Zach thought a moment. "Uh, yeah, he'll be thirteen next month."

By now they were on Mulholland Drive and approaching Zach's house. When they pulled up to the gate, the reporters stood back.

"Good," Zach said, "Sam alerted them that I'll talk to them inside."

After gaining access to the grounds, Bart stopped the SUV and allowed Zach and Emma to get out. Soon they were joined by both Sam and Emma's mom, who had obviously been watching for their arrival.

"I'm glad you two are going to be here, too," Zach said. He looked at Emma's mom. "You up to this?"

"I am if you are," she said.

Emma slipped her hand into her mother's. Her mother looked startled for a moment, but then she smiled, and Emma smiled back.

When Zach indicated he was ready, Sam walked to the gate and motioned for the reporters to come inside. Soon the drive was filled with their vehicles.

Emma's heart accelerated. She was half scared and nervous, half thrilled. From the grip of her mother's hand, she knew Zoe was far from calm, herself.

The reporters, a mix of young men and young

women—weren't there any *old* reporters? Emma wondered—began to fire questions at her dad while camera operators set up their equipment.

Her dad held up his hands until they quieted.

"Before I take your questions," he said, "I have a statement to make. He put his arm around Emma's shoulders. "I'd like you to meet my daughter, Emma Madison-Trainer." He smiled. "That's Madison-Trainer with a hyphen." He winked at Emma.

Emma tried not to show how startled she was. So that was his idea. Oh, God. What was her mother thinking? Emma was afraid to look at her.

"And standing on the other side of her is her mother, Zoe Madison, who was a singer with the band when we first started out."

More questions erupted as cameras whirred.

"Zach, Zach," called out a pretty blonde with the call letters KNBC on her mike. "Were you shocked when you found out about Emma?" She thrust the mike closer.

"Not shocked," Zach said. "Surprised. And pleased. Very, very pleased." Again he smiled at Emma.

"Why did you keep your daughter a secret for so long?" asked a skinny young man, addressing his question to Zoe.

Her mom squeezed her hand. When she answered, her voice sounded slightly amused. "I consider that a bit personal to share, don't you?"

The reporters laughed. The skinny guy shrugged.

Emma knew her mom hadn't been the least bit amused, but she was impressed that she'd managed to sound so cool and collected when she'd answered. Maybe she *wasn't* upset about the name thing.

"Tell us a little about yourself, Emma," another of the female reporters said. She gave Emma a friendly smile.

Emma looked at Zach.

He nodded. "Go ahead."

"Well, I'm a student at the School of Music at Ohio State University, and I'll be graduating in May. Other than that, there's not much to tell," Emma said.

Several other questions were called out.

"Do you play an instrument, Emma?"

"Are you a singer?"

Again, Zach held up his hand. "I'll answer that. Emma is a singer and a composer as well as a pianist. And—" He paused dramatically. "And she's going to join the band for our world tour this summer."

This announcement was greeted with another barrage of questions.

"If you all talk at once, I can't answer any of you," Zach said, laughing.

He pointed to a dark-haired woman in a purple dress who wore her hair in a long braid, something Emma had always wished she could pull off.

"My question is for Emma," the woman said.

"Emma, how long have you known that Zach Trainer is your father?"

Emma's gaze shot to her mother. Her mother gave an almost imperceptible shrug. Turning back to the reporter, Emma explained about seeing the photo on the Internet.

"And how did you feel at that moment?" the reporter continued. "Were you excited, angry with your mother for keeping this important information from you or what?"

Emma thought for a moment. Conflicting emotions warred within. She wanted to be honest, but she didn't want to hurt her mother.

"To tell you the truth," she said slowly, "I'm not sure what I felt. It was really a combination of things, but mostly excitement, I guess."

"Okay, folks," Sam said, speaking up for the first time. "That's enough for now. Zach and the band have put in a long day's work today, and I know he and Emma are both tired."

"And hungry," Zach said, grinning.

"One last question," called out a male reporter. "Hank Heffron from *Reveal,*" he added when Zach looked his way. "Have you talked to your son about his new sister?"

Before Zach could answer, Sam said, "Let's leave Will out of this, okay? Thank you all. The interview is over. Have a good evening."

And with that, he shepherded all of them into the house.

Zoe's heart had plummeted when she heard Zach say that Emma would now be known as Emma Madison-Trainer. She knew it was silly to be so dismayed, but she couldn't help it. It hurt her to have Emma take Zach's name, hyphenated or not.

I'm the one who raised her, who scrimped and saved and worked so hard. I'm the one who sat up with her when she was sick, worried about her, helped her with her homework, taught her the values she knows. I'm the one who went to her softball games, made her practice the piano, taught her to drive. Me! Not him. The only things he contributed are his sperm and his genes.

But Zoe struggled to keep her face impassive, not to show her tumultuous feelings. The last thing she wanted was for the press to say she was unhappy, angry or bitter. She'd rather die than let them see how painful Zach's announcement had been.

She wondered what other disappointments she had in store for her. For if she was sure of anything, she was certain there would be more.

"Have you made your return reservations yet, Emma?" Zoe asked as they walked upstairs to go to their respective rooms to get ready for dinner.

"No, it's an open return, but I guess I do need to call."

"When are you planning to go back? Tomorrow? Or Sunday?"

"I thought Sunday."

"Oh. Well, I'm going back tomorrow if I can get a seat. I have an open return, too."

Although her mother had tried to hide it, Emma knew her well enough to know that she was upset about Emma taking her dad's name. She sighed. She wished her dad hadn't jumped the gun, that he'd given her some time to talk to her mom and prepare her, but what was done was done. And Emma was happy about this, thrilled, in fact, that her dad *wanted* her to have his name.

Darn. She really didn't want to leave tomorrow, but this was a little thing she could do that might make her mom feel better.

Anyway, Zach was coming to Ohio soon, so it wasn't like she was really saying goodbye. And she was going to spend the entire summer with both him and Kirby…and who knew? maybe even longer.

"Okay, I'll go home tomorrow, too," she said, smiling at her mom. "If I can get on your flight."

Later, at dinner, when her mom mentioned that she needed to call the airline to see about getting the two of them on the same flight, Sam said, "Why don't you let me handle that for you?"

"That's nice of you," her mom said, "but I don't want you to have to hassle with it."

"It won't be a hassle. My assistant will take care of it. What time did you two want to leave?"

"In the morning," her mom said.

"In the afternoon," Emma said.

After a second, they both laughed. "Morning is fine," Emma said.

Her reward was a big smile from her mother, a wink from her dad and an approving nod from Sam. Even Kirby seemed to understand, for he smiled at her, too.

Now that all that was settled, Emma could hardly wait for dinner to be over. She and Kirby planned to take a drive tonight. He'd hinted that maybe she might like to see his flat—which was what the British called an apartment, he explained, although Emma had already known that.

Emma knew that if they went to his place, they would end up making love. And even though the thought thrilled her, she wasn't sure she was ready. She wanted to, and if she wasn't leaving for home tomorrow, maybe she'd do it, but under the circumstances, she thought maybe she should wait until summer. Get to know Kirby just a bit better.

You're scared. Why don't you admit it?

Okay, she was scared.

She wasn't sure why, except that this thing with

Kirby, it felt really important to her. Really special. And as such, it was something she didn't want to rush.

When they made love for the first time, she wanted it to be right. And meaningful. And not just for her. For him, too.

If he really feels something for you, if it's not just lust on his part, he'll wait....

Emma could almost hear her mother's voice cautioning her to take her time, to think before acting, to consider the consequences. Emma had always realized why her mother counseled being responsible for your actions. She'd been thinking about her own life and the mistakes she'd made, mistakes she didn't want Emma to make, too.

And why not?

Wasn't that what a good parent did? Tried to keep their children from making the same mistakes? Although, as Emma had learned a long time ago, most people didn't really learn anything until they'd made a few mistakes and suffered the consequences.

"Emma?"

Emma jumped. She'd been so lost in her thoughts she hadn't realized her dad was talking to her.

"What day is your graduation?"

"The third Saturday in May. I think it's the twentieth."

"It is," her mother said.

"You making a note of that, Sam?" her dad said.

But Sam had already whipped out his PalmPilot. Emma grinned. Her uncle—as she'd begun to think of Sam—was even more organized than her mother.

For the rest of the meal, the conversation flowed easily, centering on the new album, which would probably only take a couple more days of work before it was recorded, followed by the mixing and mastering, and the summer tour.

Finally dinner was over. Her dad stood, saying, "I'm in the mood to watch a movie. We've got two or three new ones. Who's interested?"

Emma had seen her dad's private theater and under normal circumstances would have loved spending the rest of the evening there.

"I have some phone calls to make first," Sam said. "Then I'll join you."

"I wouldn't mind watching a movie," her mom said. "How about you, Emma?"

"Um…" Emma said.

"Emma and I already have plans," Kirby said.

Emma shot him a grateful look.

"Oh," her mom said.

Her dad smiled, giving Kirby a knowing look.

In a way, it bothered Emma that her dad wasn't more like other fathers, who might have been worried about their daughter spending time with a guy she'd just met, especially one of the musicians in his band. But in another way, it was kind of nice not to have *two* people hovering and worrying. Anyway, Emma was sure her mother was doing enough of that for both of them.

After asking her mom to leave her a note so she'd know what time to get up to get ready to go to the airport, Emma and Kirby made their escape.

As they pulled out of the gate and onto Mulholland Drive, Kirby said, "Shall we go to my flat?"

Emma hesitated only a moment. "Why don't we just drive for a while? Is that okay with you?"

Kirby didn't pretend not to understand her. Instead, he gave her a sidelong smile. "Anything you want is okay with me, love. Anything at all."

When Zoe and Emma got to the airport at eleven the following morning, they discovered they'd been upgraded to first class. It was Sam's doing, of course. Zoe also knew it was Zach's money paying for it. She almost told the ticket agent she didn't want the upgrade, but the tension between her and Emma had finally seemed to ease—and Zoe didn't want to do anything to cause it to come back.

Besides, Zoe loved flying first class, which she hadn't gotten to do very often. "That sounds wonderful," she said.

"I've never flown first class," Emma said, clearly thrilled by the prospect.

So they happily settled themselves into the roomy

leather seats and got ready to be pampered. Once they were airborne, Emma closed her eyes, saying, "I didn't get a lot of sleep last night, Mom. Wake me when it's time to eat."

Zoe almost protested, but she figured she would still have plenty of time to talk to Emma after lunch and on the drive home, so she just said, "Okay."

While Emma slept, Zoe leafed through a recent copy of *Vanity Fair* and enjoyed an excellent Bloody Mary. But her thoughts kept wandering.

Last night, after Sam had given her the information about their flight, he'd told her he would be coming to Ohio in about a week. "I have some things I need to take care of here first, plus I want to be around to make sure there are no problems with the wrap-up of the album." He'd given her his e-mail address as well as his cell phone number, and she'd given him hers.

"Do you want me to do some research for you? Maybe scout out some possible homes?" Zoe'd asked.

"How about finding me a Realtor who handles upscale places?"

"Okay."

"But if you hear of any apartments in Maple Hills, let me know."

He'd smiled then, and Zoe knew he was talking about a place for him.

Remembering, especially remembering the look

in his eyes, Zoe felt the same butterflies in her stomach.

The trip to California might not have produced the outcome she'd wanted with Emma, but it had given Zoe something else—something she had almost stopped wishing for.

Maybe…just maybe…she had found a man she could count on.

Chapter Eleven

"Zoe! Tell us *everything!*"

"Yes, *everything!*"

Zoe had known she'd be in for a lot of questioning when she met her friends at Callie's the Wednesday after arriving home. "Where shall I start?" She looked at Shawn. "What did you tell them?"

"Well, they know you met Zach Trainer in New York, but that's about it. Other than what we heard on the news, of course."

So Zoe once more told her story.

"Oh, Zoe," Carol sighed when she'd finished. "It's so romantic. Just like a novel." Carol Carbone, who was one of the original members of the Wednesday night gang, devoured romance novels.

Zoe made a face. "Look, don't make this into a big tragic romance. That's not how it was. What Zach and I had was a short-lived affair. Period."

"All right, if not romantic, then *exciting*," Carol said. "You have to admit, having a baby by Zach Trainer is not your everyday, run-of-the-mill story."

"Oh, Zoe," Ann O'Brien, who was Carol's sister, said, "Aren't you just a *little* bit excited by all the attention? I mean, everyone in Maple Hills is talking about this. It's probably the most momentous thing to happen here in years."

"Yeah," Susan agreed, "I can't remember people talking like this since Eve DelVecchio married Mitch Sinclair." Susan was referring to the famous dress designer who had come back to Maple Hills for her twentieth high school reunion and ended up marrying her high school sweetheart who, incidentally, was the father of her secret baby.

"Oh, God," Zoe moaned. "This situation *is* like a romance novel. I just realized *Emma* was a secret baby!"

Her pals all laughed.

"So maybe the story will end with a happily ever after," Carol teased.

"With Zach?" Zoe scoffed. "When hell freezes over."

"How did he act when he saw you again?" Susan asked.

"Oh, he was the same old Zach. He thinks all he has to do is turn on the charm, and you'll fall at his feet."

"You don't feel *anything* for him now?" Ann asked.

"I admire the success he's attained, but that's it," Zoe said. "The thing is, Zach Trainer has never really grown up. He hasn't had to. He has lackeys who attend to his every whim. People who clean up all his messes." *Like Sam,* she thought with sudden disquiet.

"So when is he coming to Ohio?" asked Susan.

Zoe made an effort to shrug off her negative thoughts. "I don't know. His brother is coming next week, though. And that reminds me. Ann, how would you like to show him some houses?" Ann was an up-and-coming real estate agent. Zoe was pleased she could send some business her way.

"Are you kidding? I'd love it!" Ann said, grinning. "What will they want?"

"You'll have to talk to Sam about that. I'll have him call you."

"Sam," Shawn said thoughtfully. "The older brother. What's *he* like?"

Zoe wasn't ready to tell anyone about her fledgling feelings for Sam. Besides, if things didn't work out well between them—which she'd decided was likely—she didn't want anyone feeling sorry for her. So she struggled to keep her face and voice as matter-of-fact as possible. "He's not at all like Zach. He's much more down-to-earth and practical." Turning to Ann, she said, "You'll like him, Ann. He won't be demanding."

Ann was still beaming. This was a real coup for her; her reputation would receive a huge boost once word leaked out that she was shopping for a house for Zach Trainer.

"How's Emma handling all this?" Susan asked.

"Oh, she's walking on air," Zoe said, once more working to keep her emotions in check. Her eyes met Shawn's.

Shawn gave her a supportive smile.

"Well," Susan said, "it *is* exciting for her, Zoe. Imagine how you'd feel if you suddenly discovered your father was a wildly successful and famous man."

"Yeah," Zoe said glumly. "That's exactly the problem."

"What are you afraid of, Zoe?" Carol asked.

"Oh, Carol," Ann said, "surely you know."

Carol shook her head. "Maybe I'm dense, but I *don't* know."

"She's afraid Emma is going to have her head completely turned by her father and his lifestyle and that she'll leave Maple Hills for good," Shawn said.

They all murmured sympathetically, saying things like "that won't happen" and "Emma won't forget you" and "stop borrowing trouble" but Zoe knew down deep if they were in her shoes, they'd be just as worried.

Zoe turned to Susan. "I'm tired of talking about my problems. Let's talk about yours for a change. What's new with Sasha?"

Susan frowned. "I honestly don't know. After I told her she couldn't move in with me, she hasn't called. And when I call her, all I get is her voice mail. I have no idea where she's living."

Shawn put her hand on Susan's arm in a comforting gesture. "Don't worry, Susan. She's all right. She's done this kind of thing before. When she gets over being mad, she'll call."

Or when she wants something else, Zoe thought but didn't say.

The women continued to talk about Sasha for a while, but Zoe's mind drifted. In a week, Sam would be there. Zoe desperately wanted to discuss him with Shawn, see if Shawn thought Zoe was nuts to even be considering this.

I'll wait, she thought, *at least until he gets here and I see if his feelings are still the same. Maybe there won't be anything to discuss. Maybe he'll say he made a mistake and thinks it's better if he and I don't get involved. Or maybe he won't say anything at all.*

For it wouldn't surprise Zoe at all to find that, after she'd left California, he'd started having second thoughts about her. After all, she came with baggage. She'd once been his younger brother's lover. In the end, that might be a hard pill for Sam to swallow. In fact, very few men in Zoe's acquaintance would be able to handle something like that.

But Sam knows all about you now, and it hasn't seemed to present a problem so far....

Still, she wasn't going to count on anything.

That way, she wouldn't be disappointed.

Emma stood in the baggage claim area at Port Columbus International Airport. She was so nervous, her stomach felt as if it were filled with jumping beans. She'd been this way ever since finding out Kirby planned to stop over in Columbus for a couple of days before flying home to England.

His plane was late, but it was finally on the ground according to the Arrivals monitor. She wasn't sure how long it would take for him to get off and down to baggage claim, but she couldn't imagine she'd have much more of a wait. The airport wasn't huge like LAX.

She couldn't wait to see him again. They'd talked on the phone every night since Emma had been home, but talking wasn't the same as being together.

No one knew he was coming. Emma hadn't even told her mother. He would only be in town for the weekend. On Monday he was flying home to England to spend some time with his family. After that,

Emma wasn't sure. She knew his original plans had been to spend the interim between recording the new album and starting the world tour in England. Was it possible meeting her might have changed that? She guessed she'd find out soon enough. If he wasn't planning to come back to the States before the world tour started, she was determined not to let him know she was disappointed.

She wondered if she would recognize him when he *did* show up. He told her he always traveled under a fake name and wore some kind of disguise. When traveling alone, he even bought both seats in his row in the first-class section of the plane. Otherwise, he'd said, he would never have a moment's peace.

Emma realized she might have to contend with that kind of attention once more people became aware of her. She tried to imagine having to plan out her every movement—or even worrying about the strange people she'd read about who stalked celebrities. Then she laughed at herself, unable to accept the idea of herself as some kind of star.

Suddenly she saw him, although if she hadn't recognized his walk, she wouldn't have been sure it *was* Kirby, for his hair was slicked back and a dark baseball cap was pulled low over his face. Plus he wore a baggy UCLA sweatshirt over faded jeans. On his feet were beat-up sneakers, and he was carrying a battered duffel bag. He looked like a college kid.

When he spied her, he waved and started walking faster.

Emma waved back. Her heart banged against her chest like a crazy thing.

"Hello, love," he said, finally reaching her.

"H-hello," she said breathlessly.

Their eyes locked for a moment, and then he gathered her into his arms and kissed her. People jostled them as they walked past, but still they kissed.

When he let her up for air, they grinned at each other.

"God, it's good to see you," he said, keeping one arm around her and holding her close. "I missed you."

"I missed you, too." She laughed. "I almost didn't recognize you."

"Pretty good disguise, isn't it?"

"Very good. Um, what, exactly, do you call it?"

He grinned. "Slacker on holiday."

She laughed. She loved his sense of humor. "So how was your flight?"

"Except for taking off late, it was fine. I slept most of the way."

Good, Emma thought. Because if she had her way, he wasn't going to get much sleep tonight. She'd thought about this ever since leaving California, and she'd decided she didn't want to wait any longer. If Kirby still wanted her, she was willing. Not only willing, but eager.

Once more, butterflies erupted in her stomach.

Giving her a squeeze, he said, "Just let me collect my bag, then we can be on our way."

"Okay." He walked over to the carousel where the bags from his flight had just started coming down the chute. She watched the people milling around him. No one paid him any attention. It amazed Emma that they couldn't see past the worn clothing and baseball cap. There were a couple of really cute young girls waiting not far from where Kirby stood. Wouldn't they just die if they knew who was within touching distance? Emma could only imagine how they'd squeal and carry on. She couldn't help smiling over her delicious secret.

While she watched, Kirby leaned forward and grabbed a big canvas bag from the carousel. Slinging its strap over his shoulder, he turned and walked rapidly toward her.

"Let me carry your small bag," she said, reaching for it.

"I'm fine, love. Just lead the way."

It didn't take long to reach the elevator that would take them to the short-term parking lot. Five minutes later, Emma was unlocking her blue VW.

"I thought all you Yanks liked big cars," Kirby said as he tossed his bags into trunk.

"Not poor students like me. I couldn't afford to fill the gas tank of an SUV. Besides, I love my little Bug." She'd bought it used with money she'd managed to save over three summers combined with a loan from her mother.

Guilt stabbed her. Best not to think about her mother and all the things she'd done for her right now.

"Did you find me a hotel close to you?" Kirby asked once they were on their way.

This was the question Emma had been waiting for. "Well," she said slowly, willing her heart to settle down, "I didn't actually book you a room."

"You *didn't?*"

"No, I—I thought it was silly since you're only going to be here for two nights."

"So where am I staying?"

Emma kept her eyes on the road. "I thought you could just stay with me." She held her breath.

For a long moment, he didn't say anything. And then he said softly, "Are you saying what I think you're saying?"

"Yes," Emma whispered.

Reaching over, he brushed his fingers against her cheek. "How fast does this thing go, then?"

Zoe had been working long hours all week, not just to catch up from being away, but to get ahead so she could take time off next week after Sam arrived.

Getting up, she walked to her office window and stretched as she gazed out. Spring had finally decided to show its face in central Ohio, but it remained chilly compared to the weather in L.A. Still, the sun was shining and flowers were popping out everywhere and tender green leaves had begun to sprout on trees that had been barren all winter.

Only five more days and Sam would be there.

They had talked for a long time yesterday. She'd confessed how scared she still was over Emma. "I'm especially worried about this romance with Kirby. I just think that's put the kiss of death on any chance of her going back to school in September."

"Zoe, we've talked about this before," Sam had said. "This thing between them might not even last the summer. Don't attach more importance to it than there is. Remember, they're both young. Things can change quickly when you're young."

"Do you really think so?" she'd said.

"I know so."

"I hope you're right." She'd hesitated, then said, "Sam…?"

"What?"

"You'll let me know if you see anything or hear anything I *should* know, won't you?"

"Yes, but I'm not going on the tour. I told you that."

"I know, but you'll still be overseeing things. You're bound to hear what's going on, aren't you?" She bit her lip. "You know, maybe I *should* ask for a leave and go along with them."

"Zoe, Emma's twenty-two years old. You can't

babysit her forever. You've got to trust that you've given her a good upbringing and a good moral character and that she'll make the right choices."

Zoe sighed, remembering.

Was she crazy to think about starting something with Sam? Something she might not be able to control? Something that might exacerbate the situation with Emma? After all, she wanted to get Emma *away* from Zach and his influence, not make it easier for her to remain part of his sphere.

Damn, she wished she could talk to Shawn about this.

To take her mind off Sam and her conflicting feelings, she decided to give Emma a call, see if maybe she'd like to go to Pinelli's for dinner. Zoe could swing by Emma's place, pick her up, then they could eat a great meal, drink a glass or two of wine and have a real heart-to-heart talk, the kind they used to have before all this Zach business.

She wouldn't even call Emma first. She'd just go by her place and surprise her. That way Emma wouldn't be able to say no.

Five minutes later, Zoe was in the parking garage. She unlocked her car, climbed in and headed out.

It didn't take long to drive to Emma's apartment. When she got there, she smiled. She could see Emma's car in the covered parking area opposite her unit. Good. She was home.

Zoe pulled up to the gate and punched in the security code. When the gates swung open, she pulled into the complex and parked as close to Emma's apartment as she could. Emma lived on the second floor. Zoe climbed up the outside steps and stopped outside Emma's door. Then she rang the bell.

When no one answered, she rang it again. That was odd. Emma *must* be home. Why else would her car be here if she wasn't? Of course, she could have gone somewhere with a friend who drove *her* car.

Damn. Zoe had really been looking forward to seeing Emma and eating Pinelli's wonderful pasta. The last thing she felt like doing now was driving home and eating alone.

Well, you should have called her first.

Sighing, Zoe realized this really was her own fault. She *should* have called. If she had, she could have been halfway to Maple Hills by now.

Disappointed, she headed back down the stairs. When she was almost to the bottom, an older woman started climbing up. Zoe recognized her. It was Carolyn Parker, Emma's next-door neighbor and surrogate mother.

"Well, hello, Zoe," Carolyn said.

"Hi, Carolyn. How are you?"

"I'm good, except for this darned knee." She pointed to her right leg.

"What's wrong with it?"

"Same old, same old." Carolyn made a face. "Arthritis. The curse of getting older."

Zoe smiled sympathetically.

"You been visiting Emma?" Carolyn asked.

"I wanted to take her out to dinner, but she's not home."

Carolyn frowned. "She's *not?* That's funny. I saw her and a friend go up not five minutes ago."

Now it was Zoe's turn to frown. "You *did?*"

"Yeah, I did."

"Who was the friend, do you know?"

Carolyn smiled. "I've never seen him before, but he sure was cute. Emma introduced him as Kirby."

Zoe hoped her face didn't reveal the shock she felt. Kirby! Kirby *Gates* was here?

"Do you know him?"

"Yes," Zoe said. "I know him." Was it possible Emma and Kirby were inside the apartment right now? That they had purposely not answered the door? Zoe didn't want to think her daughter would ever do anything like that, and yet Zoe would have sworn Emma would never go behind her back the way she had when she'd discovered that photo of Zoe with Zach, either.

Face it, you don't know your daughter as well as you thought you did.

"Well, I'd better get inside," Carolyn said. "I left a pot of chili cooking while I went to the laundry room to throw a load of clothes in."

Zoe said an absentminded goodbye and walked to her car. Once inside, she sat thinking. Then before she could change her mind, she took out her cell phone and punched in the code for Emma's cell. Just as Zoe expected, after four rings, Emma's voice mail kicked in.

Zoe waited until the message played and she heard the beep, then she said, "Hi, Emma. I stopped by tonight to see if you wanted to go to dinner with me. But I guess you're off having fun somewhere. Give me a call when you get this message. Maybe we can do something together tomorrow or Sunday. Love you."

Then she disconnected the call.

It would be interesting to see what her daughter had to say for herself when she returned Zoe's call.

Would she tell her mother about Kirby being there?

Or would she lie to her again?

And what would Zoe do about if she did?

Emma didn't call until after ten that night. "Hi, Mom," she said.

"Hello, Emma."

"I, um, was out with some friends when you called."

"Oh? Where'd you go?"

"We were just hanging out. Got some pizza and were listening to music and talking. Nothing special."

Oh, Emma, why can't you just tell me the truth? Zoe wasn't even hurt by this latest lie. She was just angry. "You know, Emma," she said in a calm, measured tone, "I really detest being lied to."

"L-lied to? W-what do you mean?"

"I mean I know very well what you were doing tonight. I ran into Carolyn after leaving your apartment. She told me she saw you going inside your apartment…with Kirby."

For a moment, there was complete silence.

Than, in a small voice, Emma said, "I'm sorry, Mom."

"You should be."

"I won't lie to you anymore. Even if I think you won't like what I'm saying, I won't lie."

Zoe took a deep breath. *Don't say anything you'll be sorry for later.* "So how long is Kirby staying?"

"Just for the weekend. Then he's going home to England to visit his family."

"And where is he staying while he's here?"

"He's…staying at my place."

Well, I wanted the truth, didn't I? "Do you think this is wise, Emma?"

"Look, Mom, I know you mean well, but I'm twenty-two years old. I have to make my own choices, wise or not."

"Yes, I know, but it's my responsibility as your mother to point out when I think you're making the wrong choice. Emma, you barely *know* this boy."

"I know everything I need to know," she said, a defiant note creeping into her voice.

"I thought that about your father, too." The moment the words were out of Zoe's mouth, she wanted to take them back.

"You know, Mom, you said you were tired of being lied to. Well, I'm tired of you making cracks about my dad."

"I know. I'm sorry, Emma. I won't do it again." When Emma didn't answer, Zoe said, "I really *am* sorry."

Finally Emma said, "Okay. Let's forget it."

"About Kirby, I just want to say one more thing. I know you're old enough to make your own decisions, but I can't help worrying, because I don't want to see you get hurt."

Emma's voice softened. "I know. And I love you for that, but if I get hurt, that's just a part of life, isn't it?"

Sam was as nervous as a teenager on his first date. He looked at the directions Zoe had e-mailed him. If he read them right, when he reached that next stop sign, he'd be at her street.

Sure enough, the sign read Lilac Lane. And just as she'd said, her house—a pretty white frame bungalow with a front porch—had flowering lilac bushes in the front.

Pulling the nondescript rental car into her driveway, Sam turned off the ignition. He sat there for a minute just looking at the house and yard. This town, Zoe's house, her street—all were so different from L.A. And so different from what he'd pictured when he'd imagined where Zoe lived. In some ways, he was surprised.

Zoe was a sophisticated, intelligent woman who had carved out a nice career for herself. He'd have thought she'd own a contemporary home, but this house was as apple pie as you could get. He guessed he had to readjust his thinking about her. Either she had changed a lot since she was young, or she had never been the wild child Zach had made her out to be.

But did it really matter?

Wasn't the Zoe of today the woman Sam was interested in? The only one who mattered?

We all come with baggage, including me.

Opening the door, he got out of the car. He released the trunk lock; he didn't want to leave his laptop computer in the car. He was just closing the trunk when the front door opened, and Zoe stood framed in the doorway.

Sam wondered if he'd always feel like this when he saw her after being apart for a while. She literally took his breath away. Standing there, her fiery hair a cloud of copper curls, wearing jeans and a yellow shirt, she could have been twenty instead of forty.

She waved, called "Hi, Sam!" and walked toward him.

He couldn't stop smiling.

Leaving his computer on top of the car, he met her halfway. And then, not caring who might see, he pulled her into his arms and lowered his mouth to hers.

The kiss was totally unexpected. At first Zoe was so stunned, she didn't react, but a moment later, she wrapped her arms around Sam's neck and gave herself up to the tumultuous sensations.

When they finally broke the kiss, Zoe's head was spinning.

"I missed you," he said, his voice ragged. He rested his chin on top of her head.

"I missed you, too." She loved being held by him. Loved the way their two bodies fit together. Loved his strength and smell and taste.

After a long moment, he released her, holding her at arm's length. "You look wonderful."

"You need glasses." Her heart was still beating too hard. "Let's go inside. We're giving the neighbors too much to gossip about. Of course," she added with a wry smile, "my reputation is already shot now that my secret is out, so I guess it doesn't matter what else I do."

He grinned. "So I could throw you down and have my way with you, and you wouldn't object?"

She couldn't help laughing. "I may have been a little wild in my youth, but now I do draw the line at some things." She took his hand. "C'mon, let's go."

"Just let me get my computer."

Once inside, he put his computer down and drew her back into his arms.

She swallowed. "Sam…"

"What?" he said softly, his lips brushing hers. He smelled of a combination of woodsy aftershave and just plain male. It was an intoxicating mixture.

"Don't you think we should slow down a bit?"

"Why? I know how I feel. Unless…you're not sure?"

"I—" She took a deep breath, pushed away from him a bit so she could think straighter. "I don't know. Maybe I'm *not* sure."

"The way you kissed me out there said otherwise."

"Oh, I *want* you. That's not the issue. What I'm not sure about is the wisdom of what we're doing."

"Let's not think it to death, Zoe. Let's just go with the flow and see where it leads us." So saying, he drew her close again, and nuzzled her ear.

"The last time I *went with the flow,* I ended up pregnant," she murmured. But there was no force in her protest, because the last thing she wanted was for him to stop kissing her.

And when he whispered, "Where's the bed-room?" she took his hand in hers and led him up the stairs.

Chapter Twelve

Zoe wished it were dark.

Even with the slats of the wooden blinds closed, the room still had too much light in it. And Zoe didn't have a twenty-year-old body anymore.

Except for their undergarments, their clothing had been discarded and lay scattered on the floor. But even though she still wore her lacy bra and panties, Zoe felt exposed.

"You're so beautiful," he murmured. He kissed her shoulder, letting his lips trail down her neck, then into the cleft between her breasts. His hands cupped her bottom and held her firmly against him.

She could feel how much he wanted her, and it thrilled her.

"I told you before," she said breathlessly, "you need glasses."

He ignored her, and she tried to relax. But as much as she wanted to just give herself up to her feelings, she couldn't seem to stop thinking. What if he were disappointed in her? What if he'd built her up in his mind, and she didn't measure up? What if, after making love with her, he decided he'd made a mistake?

Could Zoe handle that?

I'll have to....

By now Zoe had pulled the comforter off the bed, and they were lying on top of the sheets. "Zoe," Sam whispered, "relax."

"I'm trying. I—"

Propping himself up on one elbow, he looked at her. "What's wrong? Do you want to stop?"

She swallowed. Shook her head.

"Then what?" he said.

"I—I guess I'm scared."

"Scared? Of *me?*"

"No, of course not. I'm...scared I'll disappoint you."

"You could never disappoint me, Zoe. If anything, I'm afraid I'll disappoint *you.* The truth is, it's been a long time."

"For me, too!"

He smiled, then kissed her nose. "Stop worrying, okay? Let's just agree that neither one of us has had much experience lately, so if this first time isn't one for the books, we'll do better next time."

Zoe looked up into his gorgeous eyes. He always seemed to know the right thing to say. And of course he was right. They didn't have to be perfect. Lovers rarely got it right immediately. It took time to learn what worked best. Smiling, she reached up and brought his mouth down to hers.

Before long, their undergarments became a barrier. "Let's get rid of these," he said, unhooking her bra. Soon his briefs joined her bra and panties on the floor.

He sucked in a breath as he looked at her. "You *are* beautiful. I wasn't wrong about that."

Zoe was embarrassed. It had been a long time since a man had looked at her body. And, she reminded herself yet again, it was no longer a young girl's body. *Why didn't I join the gym like Shawn wanted me to?*

She tried to distract herself by concentrating on what a magnificent body Sam had. He obviously did work out, for his chest muscles were clearly delineated, and his waistline showed no signs of middle age.

Reaching for her, his mouth captured hers once again in a heated kiss that stole Zoe's breath away. Soon they were a tangle of arms and legs and seeking mouths. Zoe felt as if she'd been ignited from within as his hands stroked and caressed and explored, finding every secret place that yearned for his touch.

And then, just as she was sure she couldn't endure another moment of wanting him, he entered her with one swift, sure stroke.

As he filled her, pushing deep, Zoe gasped, then gripped his buttocks and pressed him even closer, twining her legs around him to give him better access.

Sam.

His name sang in her heart.

Sam.

He held her tightly as ripples of pleasure began, building to a shattering climax that left her shuddering. He held her close until her body stilled, and only then did he allow himself his own release.

She could love this man.

The realization frightened her. Wonderful sex was one thing. Love was quite another. What if things didn't work out between them?

She tried to push the negative thought away, but it refused to go.

Why are you borrowing trouble? Why can't you just enjoy the moment?

But she knew why. She was frightened. And she was afraid to trust, not just her feelings for Sam, but his for her. The bottom line was, he was still Zach Trainer's brother, and he always would be.

And yet…she wanted to believe in him.

She wanted that more than anything.

Lying cradled in your lover's arms afterward, sated and still warm with pleasure, was the best part of sex, Zoe decided. She snuggled closer to Sam, who tightened his arms around her.

They were lying back to front, spoon fashion, and he had his face buried in her hair. One hand lightly cupped her breast, and every so often, he'd kiss her ear or her neck, and Zoe would sigh.

"How long are you planning to stay?" she asked after awhile.

"In your bed? Until you throw me out."

She could feel his smile against her neck, and she smiled, too. "You know what I meant."

"I don't know. As long as it takes to find the right house for Zach…and a place for me."

"Then you'll go back to California?"

"I'll have to. I'll need to meet with the lawyers and our distributor. Plus I'll need to pack up my stuff."

"Did I tell you Kirby was here over the weekend?"

"No, but I knew."

Zoe stiffened. "You *knew?*"

"Yeah. He told me he was coming."

Zoe extricated herself from his arms and sat up. Suddenly uncomfortable with her nakedness, she pulled the sheet up to cover herself. "Why didn't you tell me?"

He finally seemed to realize she was upset. "I didn't even know until Friday morning, and we didn't talk over the weekend. And to tell you the truth, by Monday when we did talk again, I had forgotten all about it."

Zoe stared at him. The happy glow from their lovemaking had faded with his revelation. "How could you forget about something so important to me?"

Now he sat up, too. "Zoe, c'mon. It's not that big a deal. I mean, you knew Kirby would probably come here once Zach arrived. What's the difference whether he came this past weekend or he comes later?"

"There's a huge difference, and if you don't see it, then you're not as smart as I thought you were. Besides, you *told* me, you *promised* me you'd keep me informed if you heard anything. You should have called me the minute you found out."

"I'm sorry. Geez—" He expelled a breath. "It never even crossed my mind."

"Obviously." She'd been right to wonder if she could trust him.

"Zoe…" he said softly. He tugged at her arm. "Come back here."

She shook her head. She was perilously near tears, and that made her mad. She hadn't cried over a man in a long time, and she wasn't about to start now. Men simply weren't worth it. Even the best of them eventually let you down. Her women friends were the only people she could trust completely. How was it she'd forgotten that?

"I suppose you also knew he was going to stay at Emma's," she said bitterly. Tossing the sheet aside, she leaned down to pick up her clothes. Still fighting tears, she put on her blouse.

"Of course I didn't know that. Damn it, Zoe, why are you acting like this?" Now he sounded mad.

Where the hell did he get off being mad? She stood, glad her blouse was long enough to cover her, and reached for her panties and jeans.

"*Acting* like this?" she said furiously. "You really want to know why I'm *acting* like this? Well, I'll tell you. Although the fact I have to spell it out tells me something I should have known to begin with." She glared at him. "I've been sick with worry from the minute I knew about Emma meeting her father, because the last thing in the world I want is for her to adopt his values and abandon everything she's learned from me. And it's obvious I was right to worry, because look what's already happened. Within just weeks, she's lied to me, she's blown off plans we've made, she's avoided me, and now she's got some kid she barely knows *living* with her.

"I thought you understood all that. I thought you sympathized and agreed with me. I thought we wanted the same things. Now I'm wondering—were you just saying you agreed with me to get me into bed?"

He stared at her. Her accusation throbbed in the air between them. "And that's what you think of me?" he said quietly.

Stonily, she met his gaze. "I think you should go."

After another long, silent moment, he threw back the sheet and got up. He didn't try to cover his nakedness. He just stood there—and, oh, God, he was a glorious sight—almost as if he were defying her to look at him, to see what it was she was pushing away. Then, very deliberately, he began to pick up his clothes and put them on.

Zoe's heart thundered in her chest. Part of her wanted to cry out and say she hadn't meant it. The other part of her knew being with Sam was too dangerous to her emotional well-being.

When he was dressed, he said, "You know, Zoe, I'm on your side. I always have been." His eyes held hers. "You're not thinking straight. If you were, you wouldn't do this."

"Maybe this is the first time I *am* thinking straight," she said stubbornly.

His jaw hardened. "You're good at finding reasons for running away from your problems, aren't you? I should have remembered that." Then he stalked out of the bedroom.

Zoe didn't move until she heard the outside door close behind him.

* * *

As always, when Zoe needed advice, comfort or reassurance she called Shawn.

"Zoe! What's *wrong?*" Shawn said.

"Oh, God, Shawn," Zoe cried, "I've made such a mess of things."

"What are you talking about? What things? Emma, you mean?"

Trying to stem the tide of tears that had begun the moment the door closed behind Sam, Zoe could hardly talk. "N-no, not E-mma."

"Then what *is* it?"

"I think I did something really stupid."

"Look, I'm coming over. We can't talk on the phone. And when I get there, I'm going to want ice cream!"

If Zoe hadn't been so upset, she would have smiled. Shawn had craved ice cream from the time her morning sickness stopped. Her husband Matt had laughed about it, saying he was spending most evenings running out to find yet another carton of Pralines and Cream.

Fifteen minutes later, Shawn's red Toyota pulled into the driveway. Five minutes after that, Zoe was blubbering on Shawn's shoulder.

Shawn waited until Zoe had calmed down. Only then did she say, "Let's go out to the kitchen. I'll have my ice cream, and you can tell me the whole story. You do have ice cream, don't you?"

Zoe sniffed. "Yes."

Once Shawn was settled at the kitchen table, Zoe began to talk. When she'd finally finished relaying the saga of her brief affair with Sam, Shawn sighed. "I wish I knew what to say."

"Just tell me if you think I was unreasonable."

Shawn slowly ate the remainder of her ice cream, then she licked her spoon and met Zoe's gaze. "I, um, do think you may have overreacted."

"But, Shawn—"

Shawn grimaced. "You asked for my opinion, Zoe."

Zoe sighed. "I know. I just…why do you think I overreacted?"

"Men occasionally do forget to tell us things."

"Not something like that. Not after he promised to keep me in the loop. Not when he knew how important it is to me to keep Emma from making a horrible mistake!"

"Look, sometimes…well, sometimes things that seem important to us don't seem as important to the men in our lives." Shawn smiled gently. "They see things differently. It's that Y chromosome thing."

"That's an excuse."

"No, Zoe, it's not. Believe me, Matt and I aren't always on the same page. The thing is, you learn to adjust. I make an effort to see his point of view, and he does the same for me." She shrugged. "Sometimes it works and sometimes it doesn't."

"So what do you do when it doesn't?"

Shawn grinned. "Then we slug it out."

Zoe smiled in spite of herself. "Verbally."

"Yes, verbally." Shawn eyed Zoe thoughtfully. "Now that we've got that out of the way, I'm wondering if his failure to tell you about Kirby being here is really what's bothering you?"

"Of course it is."

"Are you sure? Because my gut feeling is that Sam might be right. I think you *are* running scared."

Sam couldn't sleep.

He kept thinking about what had happened with Zoe and wondering if there was anything he could have done or said to change the outcome.

He knew she was frightened. That was obvious. But of what, he wasn't sure. Was it just the fear of losing Emma or was there more going on here?

Maybe he'd hold off on renting an apartment in Maple Hills. It didn't make much sense to get a place if Zoe didn't want to see him.

It might be smart to just give her some space.

At least a dozen times over the next couple of days, Zoe thought about calling Sam. She even went so far as to pick up the phone and start to press in the numbers.

But each time she disconnected the call before it went through.

What could she say?

She was still upset with him, and still not sure she'd been wrong to begin with. Yes, maybe she was scared, but that didn't lessen the fact that she'd had a legitimate right to be hurt over his failure to understand the importance of what he'd neglected to tell her.

Besides, the phone worked two ways.

And he hadn't called her.

By Tuesday she decided she wasn't going to hear from him. It hurt...it hurt a *lot*...but maybe everything had happened for the best.

Without Sam around to distract her, she could give her full attention to Emma. In fact, Zoe had begun to think she would take Zach up on his offer to travel with the band this summer. There really was no reason she couldn't take a leave of absence. Jamie France, her assistant manager, was chomping at the bit for more responsibility. She'd leap at the chance to run things while Zoe was away. And with cell phones and e-mail and laptops, Zoe would only be minutes away in the event of a crisis.

After all, what was more important? Her job? Or keeping Emma on the right track? Knowing Sam wasn't going to be accompanying the band on tour made Zoe's decision easier.

So that very afternoon, Zoe placed a call to her boss, and by the time she left for home at six-thirty, it was settled. Zoe would take a two-month leave of absence starting the first of June, and a delighted Jamie France would fill in for her while she was gone.

"Are you going to tell Emma?" Shawn asked when they talked later that night.

"Not yet."

"Do you think she'll be unhappy that you're coming along?"

"I don't know. Frankly, Shawn, I don't know much about what my daughter is thinking nowadays."

"What about Zach? Are you going to call him?"

"No, I think I'll wait till he gets here." Which got Zoe to wondering if Ann had found a house for him yet. Maybe she'd give Ann a call in the morning.

But on Wednesday morning, when Zoe came out of a meeting with her department heads, Bonnie said Ann had called her. "She wants you to call her."

"Thanks, Bonnie. Um, would you mind bringing me some coffee?"

Once she had her coffee, Zoe called Ann's office number and was told Ann had just left. Then she tried her cell. "Ann?" she said when Ann answered. Zoe could hear the sound of traffic in the background.

"Hi, Zoe. I just wanted to tell you Sam Welch and I signed a contract on a house for his brother last night."

Zoe kept her voice even. "That's good."

"I just can't thank you enough for sending this business my way."

"What're friends for?" Zoe picked up her cup and drank some of her coffee.

"And that Sam is *such* a charmer! You don't happen to know if he's attached, do you?"

Zoe nearly choked. "I, uh, no, I don't know."

"Well, like I said, he's a doll. I wonder if he'll be coming to live in the house with Zach?"

"I seriously doubt it, Ann. He just bought himself a house in California, and I know he's anxious to move into it." *That's one more reason it's best we parted ways.*

"You know, I was going to invite him to have dinner with me last night, then I lost my nerve. Now I'm sorry I didn't."

Zoe didn't know what to say. All she could envision was Sam and Ann sitting over a candlelit table somewhere. That Sam would have said yes to an invitation from Ann was a given. What red-blooded male wouldn't? Ann was a stunning blonde and didn't carry the baggage Zoe carried. At thirty-six, she was younger than Zoe, too. Of course Sam would have gone. He'd probably have made love to her, too, if she'd given him any encouragement.

Because obviously Zoe wasn't important to him.

Otherwise the phone wouldn't have been silent for the past four days.

"Maybe I'll call him today," Ann was now saying. "I don't think he's going home until tomorrow."

"Why don't you just do that?" Zoe said tightly.

For the rest of the day, the image of Ann and Sam together was all Zoe could think about.

Emma got two important phone calls Wednesday night. The first was from her father.

"We've got a house in Columbus," he said. "We can take possession on the fifteenth of the month."

Emma grinned. "That's great, Dad."

The second call was from Kirby. "I miss you already," he said. "I don't think I can stand to be away from you for two months, so I'm planning to come back to Ohio in a couple of weeks."

Emma's heart felt so full, she was afraid it might burst. "I miss you, too. Terribly."

"Good. I'd hate to think I was the only one afflicted with this disease."

"What disease?"

There was a pause. Then laughing softly, he said, "Love, Emma. Love."

Chapter Thirteen

Zoe started to tell Emma about her decision to go along on the band's summer tour several times, and each time she'd change her mind. She wasn't sure why she was hesitating. Was she afraid Emma would find some way to circumvent her plan? Or was she simply afraid Emma would now think Zoe didn't trust her? And that their relationship might be permanently damaged as a result?

Whatever the reason, Zoe kept quiet. She finally decided she would tell Emma on her graduation day. Make it seem like a happy surprise.

She also didn't tell Zach. She didn't trust him to

keep his mouth shut. Actually, she didn't trust him, period.

She knew he and his staff had moved into the house Ann had found for them the middle of April. If nothing else, Emma now kept Zoe informed of all details surrounding Zach and the band. She also told Zoe that Kirby had come back to Columbus, too.

"Why is that?" Zoe asked, even though she was sure she knew the reason. "Is Zach planning to do some work while he's here?"

"No, I don't think so," Emma answered. "The truth is, Kirby and I didn't want to wait such a long time to see each other again."

"I see."

"But he's not staying with me, Mom. He's staying at Dad's."

Zoe knew that last was meant to be a reassurance to her, but she wasn't born yesterday. Just because he was technically staying at Zach's didn't mean he was sleeping there. "That's good. Just…be careful, Emma, okay?"

"I know, Mom. I will."

They talked awhile more, and Zoe was dying to ask if Sam had been back to Columbus since Zach moved into the new house, but she didn't know how to work it into the conversation casually.

Besides, was it really important?

Hadn't Zoe already decided it was for the best that she'd broken things off with him?

"What's wrong, love?"

Emma sighed. "It's my mom."

Kirby put his arm around her again. They had been watching a Matt Damon movie on DVD when her mother called, and he left it on Pause.

"I just don't know what to say to her anymore. I know she's unhappy and feeling hurt and left out, but things can never go back to the way they were."

Kirby kissed her head. "I know."

That's what Emma loved about him. He *did* know. He understood her perfectly.

"She asked about me, didn't she?"

Emma grimaced. "You heard?"

"Some. Not everything."

"I'm sorry." Emma reached for his hand. "It's not that she doesn't like you, Kirby. She…she's just up-set about everything."

"I know."

He turned her hand so that her palm was up and raised it to his mouth. When he kissed it, Emma shivered. Oh, she loved him. She loved him so much. Each night before she fell asleep, she whispered a prayer that this thing between them would last.

"I told my mum and dad about you when I was home," Kirby said softly.

"You *did?* Wh-what did you say?"

"I said that I'd met this amazing girl and that I was very much in love with her."

Emma's heart somersaulted.

Tipping her chin so that he was looking into her eyes, he said, "I do love you, sweet Emma. You know that, don't you?"

Emma knew she was grinning like a fool. "Oh, Kirby, I love you, too! So much!" She threw her arms around him and kissed him.

Kissing led to lovemaking, and the remainder of the movie was ignored. Afterwards, nestled in his arms, Emma said, "What did your parents say when you told them you were in love with me?"

He smiled. "They want to meet you."

"They do?"

"Yes, very much."

Emma wasn't sure a person could stand being so happy. "Well, I'll be in England the end of May."

"That's what I told them, but I was hoping we could go right after your graduation. That way, we could visit with them for a week before the rest of the band shows up to get ready for the tour."

Emma knew her mother would be horribly disappointed if Emma left immediately after her graduation, but she also knew wild horses wouldn't have kept her from going. "Okay."

"And Emma? I have another idea, and I hope

you'll say yes to it, too." And then, shocking her, he reached into his pocket and pulled out a small velvet box.

Emma's hands trembled as she opened it. Inside, she found a breathtaking emerald cut diamond ring set in platinum. Speechless, she looked up.

"Will you marry me, Emma?"

Emma's eyes filled with tears. "Oh, Kirby, yes. Yes, I'll marry you."

He grinned. "That's my girl."

The first weekend in May Emma became Mrs. Kirby Gates. They didn't tell anyone. They had made arrangements ahead of time to be married by a justice of the peace whose wife and adult son stood in as their witnesses.

The decision not to tell Emma's parents was a particularly agonizing one, but it was the only one they could make. Emma knew her mother would be horribly hurt, but it couldn't be helped. Emma loved Kirby with all her heart, and she didn't want anyone to talk her out of marrying him. Once it was done, no one could change it.

They were married in the afternoon of a sunny, mild day with the promise of summer in the air. Emma wore a pale pink dress she'd found at Ann Taylor Loft and carried a small bouquet of pink roses. Kirby looked appropriately groomlike in a dark suit.

They were both so happy they couldn't stop smiling.

They spent the rest of the weekend in the bridal suite of the most expensive hotel in town. Surrounded by flowers, champagne and chocolates, they made love over and over again.

Emma kept looking at her rings, for a platinum wedding band studded with two rows of diamonds had joined her engagement ring. She turned her hand this way and that, loving the way the diamonds caught the light, but especially loving what they represented.

How did I get so lucky? she asked herself again and again. *If I hadn't seen that picture on the Internet, I'd never have known my father, and I'd never have met Kirby.* That something so important and wonderful should be the result of a chance glimpse of a photograph was almost frightening, because what if she *hadn't* seen it?

On Monday, when it was time to leave Kirby, she didn't want to. Yet she only had one more week of school, and they had a lifetime together. So she kissed him goodbye and went off to class. All day, no matter where she was or what she was doing, she thought about Kirby and wondered what he was doing and if he was thinking about her.

When her cell phone rang at three-thirty, just as her last class was over, she was already smiling before she flipped the cover open. The smile faded when she saw her mother's work number.

"Emma?" her mom said.

"Hi, Mom." She tried to smother the guilt that threatened to overwhelm her.

"Class over for the day?"

"Yeah. I was just heading for the parking lot to get my car."

"Are you going straight home?"

"I was planning to. Why?"

"Well, I was thinking...why don't you stop at the store on your way? I saw the most beautiful dress earlier today and I thought, if you like it, I'd buy it for you for graduation."

Emma swallowed. She planned to wear her wedding dress for graduation. "That's so sweet of you, Mom, but I already have a dress to wear. I bought it a couple of weeks ago."

"Oh."

The disappointment in her mother's voice made Emma feel lower than a worm. Would it have killed her to let her mother buy her a new dress? "But you know what? I can wear the dress I bought plenty of other places, so if you want to buy me a dress for graduation, I'd love to have it."

As soon as they disconnected, Emma called Kirby to tell him she'd be later than she'd thought coming home.

"Take your time, love. In fact, if you want to have

dinner with your mum tonight, go ahead. I'll be fine here on my own."

Emma had suspected she might be the luckiest girl on earth. Now she knew she was. "Have I told you lately that I love you, Mr. Gates?"

"Yes, but you can always tell me again, Mrs. Gates."

Sam almost backed out of the contract on his house. The split with Zoe had dampened his enthusiasm to such an extent, he was no longer sure he had any need for a house.

But in the end, he signed the papers and took possession, and now he was glad he had. For he loved the house. Zoe would have loved it, too, he thought sadly.

Standing on his second-story deck, he gazed out at the ocean. The setting sun had turned the water a fiery red-gold. Sam drank his wine and wished Zoe were there with him.

Once again, he debated whether or not to call her.

As much as he wanted to, he knew he'd made the right decision not to. She was the one who had sent him away. So she was the one who needed to make the first move.

If she didn't...then it wasn't meant to be.

And Sam guessed he'd learn to live without her.

The day of Emma's graduation couldn't have been more perfect. The sun shone, the spring flowers were all in bloom and the temperature that afternoon—when the actual ceremony would take place—was supposed to be in the midseventies.

This was the day Zoe had waited for. And she was determined that nothing would spoil it. Not Zach's presence. Not Kirby's presence. And not Sam's absence.

She was drinking her second cup of coffee and just finishing reading the newspaper when the doorbell rang.

Zoe frowned. She wasn't expecting anyone. She sighed. It was probably someone selling something. If so, she hoped it was one of the neighborhood children and not some pesky adult who would want to argue with her when she said she wasn't interested in their wares.

But when she got to the door, she saw Emma through the glass. Delighted, she released the dead bolt and opened the door. "Emma! What a nice surprise. Come on in."

"Hi, Mom."

They hugged and kissed, then Zoe said, "What brings you here? Shouldn't you be home getting ready for your big day?"

"I have lots of time. I wanted to come and see you first. I know we won't have a chance to talk later with all the others around."

"Have you had breakfast? I was just getting ready

to have mine." Zoe smiled. "I'll make you pancakes." As a child, pancakes had always been Emma's favorites.

"Thanks, Mom, I'm not hungry. But I'd love some coffee."

Five minutes later, they were both settled at the table. Emma drank some of her coffee, then put her cup down and took a deep breath. "There's something I have to tell you."

Everything in Zoe went still. What now?

"I know I promised you that I would seriously think about graduate school over the summer, but I've thought about it a lot already, and I've made up my mind. I'm not going to graduate school."

"Oh, Emma."

"I'm sorry, Mom, I know you're disappointed."

"I suppose now you're going to say you plan to stay with the band."

"Yes, that's exactly what I'm going to do."

"But Emma, you don't even know if you'll like—"

Emma held up her hand. "Wait. Let me finish, okay? I know Zach isn't perfect, but he is my father. I know why you felt you had to keep him away from me, but you were wrong. I want a chance to really get to know him, and staying with the band will give me that chance."

"But you'll have the summer," Zoe protested.

"Why isn't that enough? Why do you have to disrupt your entire life because of him?"

"There's more," Emma said.

And then she dropped her bombshell.

"Wanting to spend more time with my dad is not the only reason I won't be coming back for graduate school. In fact, it's not even the most important reason."

Zoe knew what was coming. Kirby. *Damn it.* Why had Emma ever *met* that boy?

"The important reason is…" Emma reached into her handbag and took something out.

Rings.

Zoe stared.

Emma slipped the rings on the ring finger of her left hand, then held it out. Gently, she said, "Kirby and I were married a week ago."

"Omigod," Zoe said. All her hopes. All her dreams for her daughter…up in smoke.

"Mom, don't look like that. I love Kirby so much. We love each other."

"You barely know him!"

"You keep saying that, but it's not true. I fell in love with him the first time I saw him." Emma's eyes filled with tears. "Sometimes you just *know*," she whispered. "And you have to trust your heart."

Zoe couldn't hold back her own tears. "I wanted you to have a better life than me."

"I will have a better life, the life I want. And it's

not too late for you to have a better life, either. You're still a young woman, and you're beautiful. You could find someone to love, too."

I did find someone to love, but I sent him away....

"Tell me you're happy for me, Mom," Emma said.

"Oh, baby, I want to be happy for you. I just don't want you to be hurt."

"And I love you for that. I do. But you can't protect me forever. I have to make my own decisions and my own mistakes."

After more hugs and tears, Emma left. Once she was gone, Zoe couldn't stop thinking about the things Emma had said. Maybe her daughter was right. About everything. Zoe especially thought about how Emma had said you have to trust your heart.

Sometimes you do *know,* she thought.

She'd known with Sam. But she'd been afraid, so she'd sent him away. And now it was too late.

"Why is it too late, Zoe?" Shawn said after Zoe had called and told her about Emma.

"Because he probably doesn't want me now."

"How will you know if you don't ask?"

Zoe didn't say anything. What if she called him and he told her to get lost?

"Don't let pride stand in your way, Zoe. You'll always regret it if you do."

Zoe had never been a coward, and she decided she

wasn't going to start now. Lots of things had scared her over the years, but she'd always faced down her fears.

So face this one!

Taking a deep breath, she picked up the phone.

He answered on the second ring.

"Sam?"

"Zoe?"

"I…oh, Sam, I've been such a fool. I was wrong to say the things I said to you. And I'm sorry. So sorry. Can you forgive me? C-can we try again?" She held her breath. *Please…*

"Where are you, Zoe?"

She blinked. Of all the things he could have said, that was the last thing she'd expected. "I—I'm at home. Why?"

"Because I'm coming over."

"Coming over? Where are *you?*"

"I'm at Zach's…in Columbus. I came in to attend Emma's graduation."

"Emma's graduation?" she repeated in confusion.

"You didn't think I'd let a little thing like an argument with her pigheaded mother stand in the way of missing my niece's college graduation, did you?" Then he chuckled. "Don't go anywhere, Zoe. I'll be there in thirty minutes."

Zoe's stomach felt like someone was tap dancing inside as she waited for Sam to arrive. He must have forgiven her. He wouldn't have called her pigheaded if he hadn't forgiven her, would he? He would have just been cold and told her to go fly a kite or something. He certainly wouldn't be coming over.

Unless he wanted to tell her off to her face.

But Sam wasn't like that.

Was he?

She paced around, her heart jumping every time she heard a car coming down the street.

Finally a silver Honda Accord pulled into her driveway. Watching through the window, Zoe saw Sam climb out. He looked achingly handsome in jeans and a blue knit shirt the exact color of his eyes.

Zoe took deep breaths to calm herself, then opened the door.

She stood in the doorway, and their eyes met.

I love you....

For a moment, he didn't move. Then, several long strides later, he was climbing the steps to the porch.

"I just have one question," he said, taking her arm and propelling her back into the house. He closed the door behind them. "Do you love me, Zoe?" He was still holding onto her arm.

Zoe was so stunned, she didn't say anything.

"Because I love you," he said, "and I want us to be together."

To Zoe's everlasting embarrassment, she started to

cry. "I—I was so afraid you wouldn't want me anymore."

"Ah, Zoe," Sam said. He gathered her into his arms and held her close. Gently wiping her tears away with his hand, he kissed her. "I could never say that. No matter what you did or said."

They kissed again, and this time Zoe wrapped her arms around him and poured her heart and soul into the kiss. When they finally broke apart, she said, "I do love you, Sam. More than I ever imagined I could love anyone. And I want us to be together, too."

"Does that mean you'll marry me?"

"Are you *asking* me to marry you?" She grinned. "If you are, I want a proper proposal. I've never been married, so I want to do this right."

Sam rolled his eyes. "You drive a hard bargain, woman. Okay, here goes." Dropping to one knee, he took her right hand in his. "I love you, Zoe Madison, and I want you for my wife. Will you marry me?"

"Hmm," she said. "Do I have to promise to love, honor and obey?"

"I doubt anyone could get you to promise to obey," he said dryly.

"Smart aleck." But she was laughing. "Okay, if I don't have to promise to obey, then yes, I'll marry you."

A long time later, twined in each other's arms in Zoe's bed, Zoe thought about what their life together would be like. She knew they still had problems. Like their careers. And where they'd live. And Sam's ties to Zach.

But she was confident that somehow, together, as long as they loved and respected each other, they would work them out.

* * * * *

*Coming next month: the third book
in the* CALLIE'S CORNER CAFÉ *series,
SHE'S THE ONE,
which tells Susan's story!*

Since when did life ever tell you where you were going?

Sometimes you just have to dip your oar into the water and start to paddle.

THE
SUNSHINE
COAST
NEWS

KATE AUSTIN

If you enjoyed what you just read,
then we've got an offer you can't resist!

Take 2 bestselling love stories FREE!

Plus get a FREE surprise gift!

Clip this page and mail it to Silhouette Reader Service™

IN U.S.A.
3010 Walden Ave.
P.O. Box 1867
Buffalo, N.Y. 14240-1867

IN CANADA
P.O. Box 609
Fort Erie, Ontario
L2A 5X3

YES! Please send me 2 free Silhouette Special Edition® novels and my free surprise gift. After receiving them, if I don't wish to receive anymore, I can return the shipping statement marked cancel. If I don't cancel, I will receive 6 brand-new novels every month, before they're available in stores! In the U.S.A., bill me at the bargain price of $4.24 plus 25¢ shipping and handling per book and applicable sales tax, if any*. In Canada, bill me at the bargain price of $4.99 plus 25¢ shipping and handling per book and applicable taxes**. That's the complete price and a savings of at least 10% off the cover prices—what a great deal! I understand that accepting the 2 free books and gift places me under no obligation ever to buy any books. I can always return a shipment and cancel at any time. Even if I never buy another book from Silhouette, the 2 free books and gift are mine to keep forever.

235 SDN DZ9D
335 SDN DZ9E

Name	(PLEASE PRINT)	
Address	Apt.#	
City	State/Prov.	Zip/Postal Code

Not valid to current Silhouette Special Edition® subscribers.

Want to try two free books from another series?
Call 1-800-873-8635 or visit www.morefreebooks.com.

* Terms and prices subject to change without notice. Sales tax applicable in N.Y.
** Canadian residents will be charged applicable provincial taxes and GST.
   All orders subject to approval. Offer limited to one per household.
   ® are registered trademarks owned and used by the trademark owner or its licensee.

SPED04R   ©2004 Harlequin Enterprises Limited

Silhouette

SPECIAL EDITION™

A BACHELOR AT THE WEDDING

by *KATE LITTLE*

March 2006

The oldest—and singlest—of five sisters
in a zany Italian family, Stephanie Rossi
was too down-to-earth to let her boss,
heartthrob hotelier Matt Harding,
sweep her off her feet. Or was she?
She was about to find out—
at her own sister's wedding....

Silhouette®

COMING NEXT MONTH

SPECIAL EDITION

SSECNM0206